The right of the
University of Cambridge
to print and sell
all manner of books
was granted by
Henry VIII in 1534.
The University has printed
and published continuously
since 1584.

# Cambridge University Press

Cambridge    New York    Port Chester    Melbourne    Sydney

**Project co-ordinators**     Jim Hudson
*General Adviser (Science)*

Jon Sargent
*Director*
*Science Education*
*Development Unit*

**Key stage 3 co-ordinator**  Wendy Jeffery
*Advisory Teacher for Science*

**Authors**

Laboratory matters:    Wendy Jeffery
*Science Education Development Unit*

Jon Sargent
*Science Education Development Unit*

Bodyworks:    Robin Holloway
*Steyning Grammar School*

Wendy Jeffery
*Science Education Development Unit*

Weatherwatch:    Mark Shahparaki
*Thomas Bennett Community College*
*Crawley*

Stephen Wright
*Warden Park School, Cuckfield*

Move it!:    Garry Archer
*St Paul's RC School*
*Haywards Heath*

Jon Sargent
*Science Education Development Unit*

Derek Slack
*Science Education Development Unit*

Living and changing:    Joy Bannister
*Warden Park School, Cuckfield*

Julian Sims
*Science Education Development Unit*

Published by the Press Syndicate of the
University of Cambridge
The Pitt Building, Trumpington Street,
Cambridge CB2 1RP
40 West 20th Street, New York, NY 10011, USA
10 Stamford Road, Oakleigh, Melbourne 3166,
Australia

© West Sussex County Council 1991

**British Library cataloguing-in-publication data**
Key stage 3
Y7
Pupil's book
1. England. Schools. Curriculum subjects: Science
I. Jeffery, Wendy   II. Series
507.1042

ISBN 0 521 39622 0

First published 1991

Designed by Pardoe Blacker Publishing Ltd,
Shawlands Court, Newchapel Road, Lingfield,
Surrey RH7 6BL
Illustrated by Annabelle Brend, Dawn Brend, Neil Bulpitt, Chris Forsey, Mike Gordon, John Hutchinson, Frank Kennard, Jenny Mumford, Keith Palmer, Peter Sarsen, Jon Williams, Paul Williams
Indexed by Indexing Specialists, 202 Church Road, Hove, East Sussex BN3 2DJ

Printed and bound in Spain by Mateu Cromo.

NEW HORIZONS

science 5~16

XYZ

Cambridge

# Contents

# Introduction

## A message from the authors of New Horizons

This book will help you with the work you will cover in science this year. It consists of five modules:

- *Laboratory matters*
- *Bodyworks*
- *Weatherwatch*
- *Move it!*
- *Living and changing*

Although there are five separate titles, you will find that ideas from one also appear in others. Each spread contains some ideas for you to think about and to discuss with your friends and teacher, as well as suggestions for practical work. These are denoted by ■ in the text.
**N.B.** Where you see this symbol (left) you will need to take more care. If you are not sure why, ask your teacher.

In *New Horizons* there is great emphasis on practical work. We believe that being a scientist means doing science and understanding why you are doing that practical work. We have described the 'doing' of science by means of the chart on the opposite page, which we have called the 'exploration machine'. You may have met this chart before. The 'gear wheels' show the sequence of processes you should follow as you investigate a problem. Scientists operate in very similar ways – going through the stages of describing a problem, making a plan, taking action to follow the plan, interpreting (or thinking about) their results and reporting what they have found out to other people.

On each activity there is a 'gear wheel' from the 'exploration machine'. It is there to indicate to you which scientific skill you will be concentrating on in that particular activity. You will, of course, use many skills in the activities, but we think it is a good idea for you to practise *one* skill in each activity, rather in the way that a tennis player might practise one skill for a while before developing another.

In each module, there is a complete exploration for you to undertake. An exploration is an activity with a difference. You will probably need most of the skills that you have practised. You will certainly need some of the knowledge about science that you have acquired, together with perseverance and determination to solve the exploration and find an answer. Your teacher will encourage you to use the 'exploration machine' to help you plan and carry out your task. At the end of the task, you will be required to report on it, perhaps by writing about it or by talking to your class.

We hope you will enjoy *New Horizons*. We liked writing the books, and the pupils of West Sussex enjoy using them! We believe that science is best understood by doing it and by talking about it. Through an understanding of science you will become more aware of the world around you and better able to use your knowledge and skills in real-life situations.

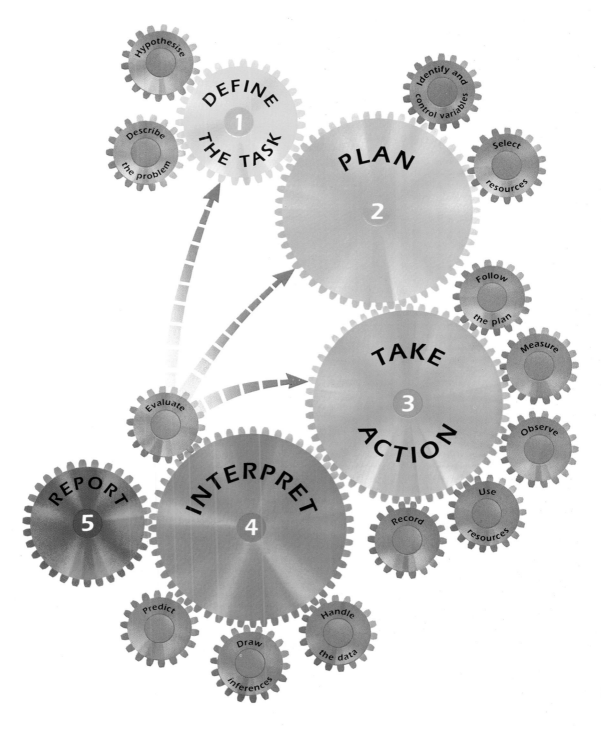

# Being a scientist

## What is science?

Science usually means knowing about the world around us. At school, you will investigate some of the questions that have puzzled scientists for a long time, such as:

- How do things fall?
- How does a human body work?
- What causes weather?
- Why do fish have gills?

Only recently have answers to questions like these been found. The exciting thing about science is that there is far more to be found out than we have already discovered! Perhaps there are some questions you would like to know the answers to.

## Who is a scientist?

Perhaps you have heard of geologists, astronomers and botanists.

- Can you find out what kind of science these people investigate and the sort of questions they ask?

There are many different kinds of scientist.

- Look at the pictures of scientists working.
- What do you think they are doing and where are they doing it?

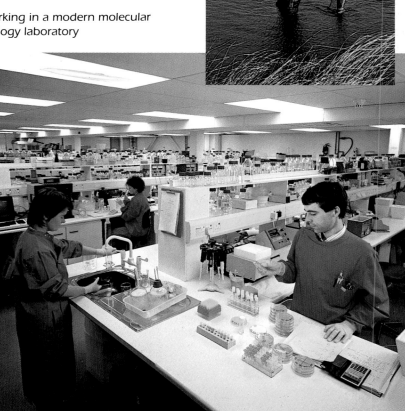

A scientist working in the field

Working in a modern molecular biology laboratory

All scientists have one thing in common; the way in which they work. It is called the 'scientific method'. In school you will learn how to work scientifically and you will use this method of working at home as well as at school.

You may already be used to working scientifically and you have seen the 'exploration machine' at the front of this book. As a scientist, you will learn the skills of science. You will learn to ask questions, make plans, carry out your plan safely, and interpret what you have found out. You will also need to report your discoveries. You will often have to work with other people. Scientists usually work in teams, so co-operation with other people is important.

Although the pictures show scientists working in a variety of places, you will do much of your science in a laboratory, because when gas, water and electricity are needed for investigations, this is the best place to be.

In this module, you will learn some of the skills of science and also about materials and how they are used.

## *Being safe and sensible*

Careless behaviour in a laboratory can cause accidents. Your school laboratory will only be a safe place for working if everyone behaves sensibly and sticks to a few sensible rules.

- Look carefully at the picture.
- Discuss whether or not these pupils are behaving sensibly.
- What might happen to the pupils if they do not behave sensibly?

An astronomer at the controls of the 2.5 m Isaac Newton telescope on La Palma in the Canary Islands. The dotted line on the screen shows the path of light through the telescope

- Make a list of safety rules for your laboratory.
- Design and make a safety poster which tells other pupils about one of the rules.

Draw inferences

# Finding out about apparatus

thermometer

measuring cylinder

beaker

## Name that piece!

The pictures show everyday scientific equipment, or apparatus. Use the pictures to name the items your teacher gives you. Later on, you will learn to handle them safely and with confidence.

## Drawing apparatus

Scientists always make a record of their investigations.

Drawing a clear, accurate, labelled diagram is a good way of showing how apparatus is assembled and used. **Data sheet D1.2** shows how some pieces of apparatus are drawn.

■ Draw a clear, labelled diagram of the apparatus in the photograph.

Remember not to draw retort stands or heatproof mats.

10

magnifier

spatula

test-tubes

gauze

test-tube rack

tripod

boss head

Bunsen burner

clamp

heat proof mat

filter funnel

delivery tube

retort stand

pestle and mortar

stirring rod

11

# Heating things

Until the year 1854, gas made from coal (coal gas) had been used mainly for lighting. Coal gas was not used for heating because its flame did not give out much heat.

In 1854, Robert Bunsen (1811–99), a German scientist, decided that a much hotter flame was possible. His idea was to mix air with coal gas just before it burned. This gave less light but more heat. The type of burner which does this is known as a Bunsen burner.

Bunsen burners now burn natural gas or calor gas.

## Using a Bunsen burner

Three different types of flame are possible with a Bunsen burner.

The different flames are made by turning the collar.

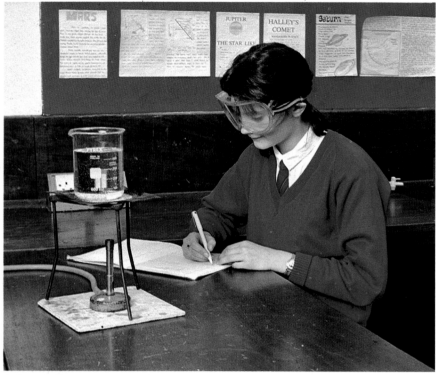

Safe use of a Bunsen burner in the laboratory

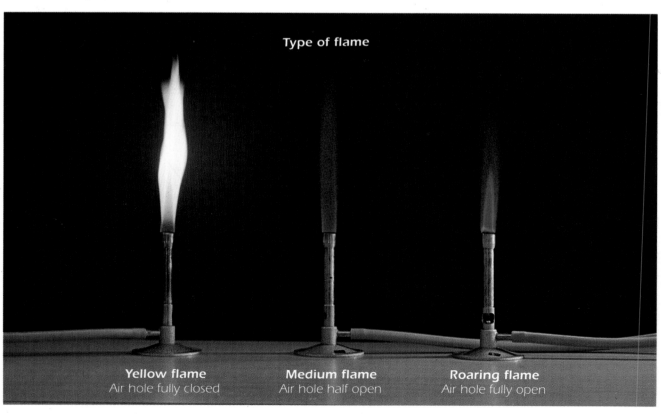

Type of flame

**Yellow flame**
Air hole fully closed

**Medium flame**
Air hole half open

**Roaring flame**
Air hole fully open

## Lighting the Bunsen burner

- Close the air hole.
- Light a splint.
- Apply the lighted splint from the side to the top of the burner, as shown below.
- Turn the gas on.

Your burner should be showing a yellow flame.

## Which flame shall I use?

collar
jet
air hole

- Set up the apparatus as shown on the opposite page.
- Light your Bunsen burner and adjust it to burn with a medium flame.
- Time how long it takes to boil a beaker containing 50 cm$^3$ of water using this flame.
- Remove the Bunsen burner and, when the beaker is cool enough to handle, exchange it for the next one.
- Repeat the experiment by adjusting your Bunsen burner to give a roaring flame.

Follow the plan

Your teacher will perform the same experiment using the yellow flame.

- Put your results in a table like the one below.
- Draw a labelled diagram of your apparatus.
- Which flame was the worst for heating the water?
- Why is the yellow flame sometimes called the safety flame?

| Type of flame | Time taken to boil water | Other observations |
| --- | --- | --- |
| Roaring | | |
| Medium | | |
| Yellow | | |

13

# What is matter?

Everything in the world, including ourselves and all the things around us, is made of something which we call **matter** or **material.**

The buildings we live in, the clothes we wear, the food we eat, the water we drink and the air we breathe, are all made of matter.

## Solids, liquids and gases

**Matter** can be found in three different forms or **states** – the solid state, the liquid state and the gas state.

■ Discuss what you think the words solid, liquid and gas mean.

Words such as 'hard', 'flexible' and 'runny' describe materials. Scientists call them the properties of the material. The statement 'glass is transparent' describes the property (transparent) of the material (glass).

■ Can you think of some properties that all solids have?

■ What can you say about their size and shape?

■ Ask yourself the same question about liquids and gases.

■ How do you decide whether something is a solid, liquid or a gas?

■ Compare your ideas with the table on **data sheet D1.4.**

**LABORATORY MATTERS**

## What's the state?

The picture shows objects made from different materials which have different properties. They can be sorted into groups using their properties.

When scientists sort things into different groups, they are **classifying** them.

Classifying helps scientists to identify patterns in their data.

■ Use your own ideas and the information on **data sheet D1.4** to classify the objects and materials you have been given as solids, liquids or gases.

■ Devise a way of recording your ideas.

Record

15

## 1.5 Moving particles

### Particle arrangement

You already know that solids, liquids and gases have different properties, but why do they behave as they do?

All matter is made of very tiny particles called **atoms.** These particles are so small that they cannot be seen, even through the most powerful optical microscope!

Although we cannot see them, we do know that these particles are always moving, sometimes slowly, sometimes more quickly.

In solids, particles are closely arranged in regular patterns and do not move about, although they do **vibrate** (move back and forth) slightly. This is why solids have a definite shape. Particles in liquids are not arranged in a regular way. They are free to move about, but they do stay close to each other. This is why liquids are runny and can be poured.

In a gas, the particles can move away from each other. They are able to move very quickly. They are not held close to other particles at all.

When a substance is heated, the particles in it move more quickly because they have more energy.

■ What do you think will happen to the particles when the substance cools down?

## Handling substances

Only use small amounts of substances.

■ Observe the three substances you have been given carefully. How would you describe them?

■ Copy the table and record your observations in the first two columns.

| Name of substance | Before heating | During heating | After heating (cool) |
|---|---|---|---|
|  |  |  |  |

Heating a substance safely

## Heating substances

The picture shows the correct way to heat substances.

■ Very gently heat a small amount of one of the substances in a boiling tube. Make sure you use the correct flame for gentle heating.

■ Observe what happens carefully. Allow the tube to cool before replacing it in the rack and continue to observe.

■ Record *all* your observations in the table.

■ Repeat the activity using the other substance.

Your teacher will heat a third substance for you to observe.

When substances change from one state to another as a result of heating or cooling we say they have 'changed state'. They are still the same substance and made from the same particles. **Data sheet D1.5** will help you to understand more about this.

■ Explain what you think has happened in the three substances that you heated using words like 'particles', 'heat', 'move', 'solid', 'liquid', 'gas', and 'state' to help you. Drawings may help your explanation.

Follow the plan

17

# Separating mixtures

Materials in the same or in different states are often mixed together. Some examples of mixtures are:

- gases: air – a mixture mainly of nitrogen and oxygen
- liquids: vinegar – a mixture of ethanoic acid and water
- solids: brass – a mixture of two metals, copper and zinc. A mixture of two metals is called an **alloy**. Use some other sources of information to find out more about alloys.

To separate substances from mixtures, we use our knowledge of their properties. One property of solid substances which is very useful for separating mixtures is its **solubility** or how easily it dissolves.

When sugar is mixed with water it dissolves. It is said to be **soluble.** Solids that do not dissolve are said to be **insoluble.**

■ Discuss what you think happens to the particles of sugar when they dissolve in water.

## Filtration

Filtration is a way of separating insoluble solids from liquids, using a **filter** or fine strainer. When peas are strained using a colander they are being separated from the water. This happens because the holes in the colander are smaller than the peas.

A coffee filter separates the solid coffee grains from the water. The filter paper has millions of tiny holes which are too small for large coffee grains to pass through. The tiny particles of coffee which give it its taste can pass through to flavour the water and make the coffee we drink.

■ What is being filtered in the pictures above?

For filtering in the laboratory, we use a filter funnel and filter paper. We call the liquid which passes through the filter paper the **filtrate** and the solid which is left on the paper the **residue.**

18

## Filtered out

- Set up the retort stand, filter funnel and conical flask as shown in the photograph.
- Wet the filter funnel.
- Fold the filter paper and place it in the funnel.
- Copy the table into your book.
- Pour 25 cm³ of the sandy water slowly into the filter paper. Do not let the water go over the top edge of the filter paper.
- Time how long it takes for the liquid to pass through the filter paper.
- Record your observations in the table.
- Using a new filter paper each time, repeat the experiment for the muddy water, the chalky water and the milk.
- Draw and label a diagram of the apparatus.
- Why do you think some mixtures take longer to separate than others?
- Why do you think the filter paper was unable to remove the white substance from the milk?

Draw inferences

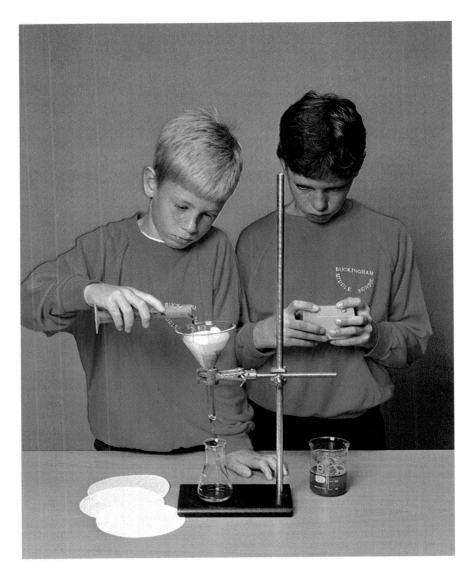

| Mixture | Time for filtrate to pass through filter paper | Description of filtrate | Description of residue |
|---------|-----------------------------------------------|-------------------------|------------------------|
| Sandy water | | | |
| Muddy water | | | |
| Chalky water | | | |
| Milk | | | |

# 1.7 Evaporation

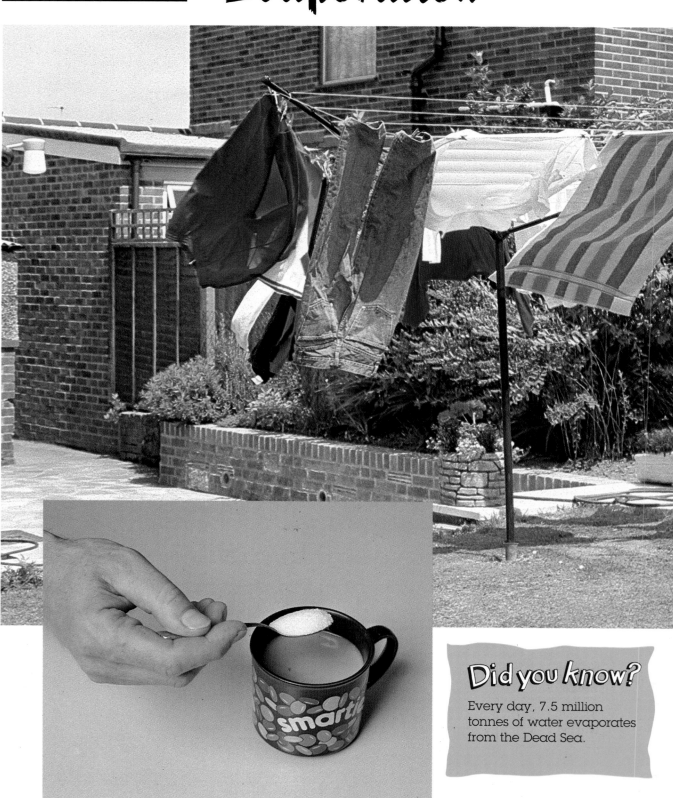

## Did you know?

Every day, 7.5 million tonnes of water evaporates from the Dead Sea.

Is tea a solution? What is the solute? What is the solvent?

Workers in Sri Lanka raking salt into piles as sea water evaporates from a shallow salt pan

Why do clothes dry more quickly on a windy day?

## Dissolving

What happens to sugar when it is added to water? It seems to disappear, but has it really? The sugar has dissolved.

A solid that dissolves is called a **solute.** The liquid it dissolves in is called a **solvent.** The solute and solvent together are called a **solution.**

## Separating salt

Seawater has common salt dissolved in it as well as other soluble substances.

In some dry parts of the world, people do not have an adequate fresh water supply. Some of them live near the sea.

■ What problems do these people have to overcome before they can use the sea to supply fresh water?

When salt dissolves in water, salt is the solute and water is the solvent.

■ Make a solution of common salt in water.
■ Using the 'exploration machine', plan an investigation to separate the salt from the water. Show your plan to your teacher.
■ Carry out the plan.
■ Report what happened during your investigation.

What happens when you dry your hair?
■ Discuss with your friends the most efficient way of getting your hair dry. What does drying your hair have in common with the pictures on this page?
■ Look at **data sheet D1.5** and discuss with your friends what happens to the liquid water in the pictures above.

# Separating pigments

Have you ever wondered why flowers are different colours or why people have different coloured eyes? Soluble substances called **pigments** are responsible for the colours of many things. You may have mixed paints to make different colours. The final colour is a mixture of different pigments. We can separate mixtures of pigments by a method called **chromatography.**

## What colour is black ink?

- Half fill a beaker with water.
- Cut a strip out of a filter paper leaving the strip attached at the middle (see diagram).
- Using the end of a glass rod, put a small drop of ink in the middle of the filter paper. Allow it to dry.
- Place the filter paper over the top of the beaker, dipping the end of the strip into water.
- Watch what happens carefully and record your observations clearly and accurately.
- How many pigments did you separate from the black ink?

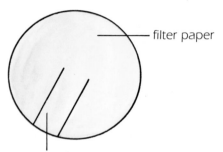

filter paper

cut strip of paper leaving one end attached

ink

clean water

**LABORATORY MATTERS**

## Separating plant pigments

Not all plant pigments are soluble in water; some will only dissolve in other solvents such as ethanol and propanone.

In this activity, you will investigate which is the best solvent to dissolve different plant pigments.

■ Choose one part of a plant for investigation.

■ To extract the pigment, grind up the plant tissue in a pestle and mortar with a small volume of water and pour the liquid into a test-tube.

**SAFETY**

There must be no naked flames in the room during this activity.

■ Repeat using the other solvents instead of water.

■ How will you decide which is the best solvent?

■ How will you make sure your test is fair?

■ Devise an appropriate way to record your observations.

■ Report what happened during your investigation.

You could carry out the investigation using different plant parts.

■ Which is the best solvent for each of the pigments you have tested?

■ If plant pigments were soluble in water, what would happen when it rained?

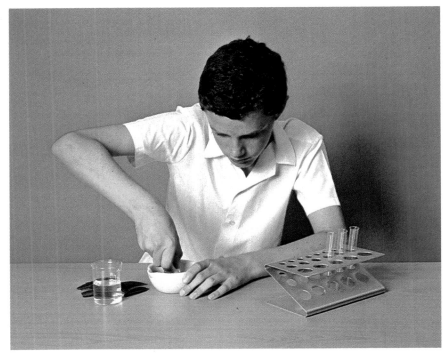

Grinding plant tissue with a pestle and mortar

# Acids and alkalis

There are many common substances that contain chemicals called **acids**. Acids give these substances their sharp, sour taste. You probably know that acids are corrosive. This means that they may attack and 'eat away' substances such as metals and may burn your skin. Vinegar contains ethanoic (acetic) acid. Lemons and grapefruit contain citric acid. A bee sting is acid.

One type of indigestion, called acid indigestion, is due to the presence of too much acid in the stomach. It can usually be cured by taking indigestion tablets which neutralise (or cancel out) the acid.

## Neutralisers

In the laboratory, acids can be neutralised by chemicals called **alkalis**. Acids and alkalis can neutralise each other if they are mixed in the right amounts. Washing soda is a common alkali, and so are wasp stings!

A **neutral** solution is neither acidic nor alkaline.

■ What everyday chemicals would you use to neutralise:
● a wasp sting?
● a bee sting?

The table below gives some commonly used laboratory acids and alkalis. These colourless liquids are often used in experiments. You will understand more about them later in your course.

Common alkaline substances. Can you name the alkalis they contain?

| Name of acid | Name of alkali |
|---|---|
| hydrochloric acid | sodium hydroxide |
| sulphuric acid | calcium hydroxide |
| nitric acid | ammonium hydroxide (ammonia solution) |

**SAFETY** ⚠️
Laboratory acids and alkalis are chemicals that must be used with extreme care. Never use them unless told to do so by your teacher.

## Did you know?

The acid in the human digestive system is strong enough to dissolve an iron nail.

Common acidic substances. Can you name the acids they contain?

**LABORATORY MATTERS**

## Indicators

**Indicators** are dyes that change colour when they are added to acids or alkalis. The first indicators used were natural dyes extracted from plants. Universal indicator is a mixture of several dyes. It produces a range of different colours when acids and alkalis are added to it. By matching the colour to a chart, we can see how strong an acid or alkali is.

## pH and the pH scale

As well as using a scale of colours, we can use a scale of numbers, called the **pH scale**, to measure acid or alkali strength.

A neutral substance has a pH of 7. Acids have pH values below 7. Alkalis have pH values greater than 7.

## Using universal indicator

- Label your six test-tubes A to F.
- One quarter fill the tubes as follows:
  - **A** ammonium hydroxide
  - **B** citric acid
  - **C** sodium carbonate
  - **D** hydrochloric acid
  - **E** sulphuric acid
  - **F** distilled water
- Test each solution with universal indicator paper.
- Match the colour of the paper to the universal indicator chart to find the pH of each solution.
- Record your observations for each solution in the table.

Record

Universal indicator colours and pH scale. (Look at your school universal indicator chart for accurate colours.)

| Colour | pH | |
|---|---|---|
| red | 1 | strong |
| orange | 2 | |
| | 3 | **acids** |
| | 4 | |
| orange yellow | 5 | |
| yellow | 6 | weak |
| yellowish green | 7 | neutral |
| greenish yellow | 8 | weak |
| green | 9 | |
| bluish green | 10 | |
| | 11 | **alkalis** |
| blue | 12 | |
| | 13 | |
| violet | 14 | strong |

| Solution | Colour of universal indicator paper | pH | Acidic or alkaline | Strength of acid or alkali |
|---|---|---|---|---|
| A | | | | |
| B | | | | |
| C | | | | |
| D | | | | |
| E | | | | |
| F | | | | |

# 1.10 Measuring matter

Enlargement of meniscus. When measuring the volume of liquids always read from the bottom of the meniscus

## Measuring liquids

- Measure the mass of a 250 cm³ measuring cylinder.
- Remove the measuring cylinder from the balance and measure 200 cm³ of water into it.
- Measure the mass of the water and the measuring cylinder together. What is the mass of the 200 cm³ of water? Show your calculations.
- Repeat your measurements using cooking oil instead of the water.
- Calculate the mass of 200 cm³ of cooking oil.
- Compare the mass of the same volume of water and oil. Were they the same or different?
- Record what you have discovered.

## Did you know?

Solids are not always denser than liquids. Ice is less dense than water. This is why icebergs float in the sea. Pumice, a kind of volcanic rock, can float on water too; the only rock to do so.

**Precisa** 1600C

**LABORATORY MATTERS**

## Measuring solids

You can also use a measuring cylinder in order to find the volume of a solid.

■ Measure 50 cm³ of water into a 100 cm³ measuring cylinder. Place a pebble in the water and then read off the new volume.

■ Calculate the volume of the pebble. Show your calculations.

Your teacher will provide blocks made from a range of materials.

■ Measure the mass of each of the blocks.

■ Use a similar method as before to find the volume of each of the solid blocks.

■ Record all the data about the blocks in a table like the one shown below.

■ What can you say about the volume of the blocks? Do they all have the same mass?

Materials which have the same volume may not have the same mass. You have seen that this is true for solids and liquids. Materials that have different masses for the same volume are said to differ in **density.** Water is denser than cooking oil. Why?

■ Predict what will happen if you mix together water and cooking oil.

■ Test your prediction and draw a labelled diagram to record your observations.

■ Which of the blocks had the highest density? Look at the table to help you. How do you know this?

■ Use your ideas about particles to explain why different materials have different densities.

| Block material | Volume (cm³) | Mass (g) |
| --- | --- | --- |
|  |  |  |
|  |  |  |
|  |  |  |

Measuring gases

## Measuring gases

Your teacher will set up the apparatus and demonstrate this activity to you.

■ Make an hypothesis about what will happen to the mass reading when the air in the container is removed using a vacuum pump. An hypothesis means that you not only make a guess about what may happen, but also why it happens.

Hypothesise

Your teacher will carry out the evacuation.

■ Can you explain what happens?

■ What does this activity tell us about air? (Remember that air is a mixture of gases.)

■ Report what happened in this activity to include an explanation of your observations.

# Salt from where?

We take table salt for granted, but where does it come from? People in some hot countries can get salt from the sea by evaporation. In England, large amounts of rock salt are found deep underground in Cheshire. Sources of rock salt consist of a mixture of salt and rocky fragments.

Imagine that you are a research chemist working for Salto, a large salt-purifying firm. There are two sources of supply for the rock salt, which is the raw material from which Salto makes pure table salt. The cost of buying salt from X or Y is the same, but one contains more pure salt than the other.

*Mechanical cutters extracting salt in the Winsford salt mine, Cheshire, UK*

**LABORATORY MATTERS**

Salt in a drying kiln at the Lion salt works, Cheshire, UK

## Exploration: Choosing the best source

■ Your task is to plan and carry out an exploration to help you discover which of the two sources of supply is the more economic to use.

**Remember:**
● Follow the 'exploration machine'.
● Report your exploration under the headings:
*Task, Plan, Action, Interpretation.*

# The microscope

The microscope is a very useful instrument. It makes things appear larger – in other words it magnifies. No-one is exactly sure who invented the microscope, but it was in use in Europe by about 1600.

Scientists of the time were very excited because they were able to see things that people had never seen before. They were keen to improve this new device so that they could see in even more detail.

Marcello Malpighi (1628–94) was born in Italy. He studied the lung of a frog under his microscope and discovered the tiny blood vessels that are known as capillaries.

In Holland, Anthony van Leeuwenhoek (1632–1723) developed a more powerful microscope through which he could see the smallest plants and animals in pond water.

Fig: 5.

Fig: 6.

A microscope (left) made by English scientist Robert Hooke in 1663. Through his microscope, Hooke saw that cork was made up of small 'boxes', which he called cells (above)

## *Using a microscope*

- Look at **data sheet D2.1**.
- Compare the microscope on the sheet with your own. You should learn the names of the different parts.
- If your microscope has a built-in light source, switch on the light. Otherwise, adjust the mirror until you can see the most light through the tube. You can now use your microscope to examine something from the selection your teacher will provide.
- Place what you have chosen to examine on a microscope slide.
- Put the slide on the stage so the material is over the hole and secure the slide with clips.

- Check that the nosepiece is turned to the low-power objective lens.
- Look from the side, with your eye level with the stage and, turning the focussing knob, bring the lens and the slide close together – make sure they do not touch!
- Now, look down the eyepiece and, turning the focussing knob, slowly move the objective lens away from the slide until you can see a clear image. The material on the slide is now in focus.

When you have finished, always leave your microscope clean and put it away.

You should adjust the mirror to the brightest position.

Follow the plan

# What are cells?

All living things are made up of tiny units called **cells.** Some animals are so small they are made of only one cell, but most **organisms** (living plants and animals) are made of many different cells. Most cells have certain things in common. Nearly all cells have a 'control centre' called a **nucleus** which controls everything going on in the cell.

The diagrams below show an animal cell and a plant cell. Although they both have a nucleus, there are some differences between them.

■ Which features do plant and animal cells have?
■ Which features do only animal cells have?
■ Which features do only plant cells have?

## Features of cells

The **cytoplasm** is where the cell stores and makes chemicals.

The **cell membrane** holds the cell together. It is very thin and allows some food particles and oxygen to pass through it.

The **cell wall** of plant cells is a rigid structure around the cell. It allows most things to pass through it.

**Chloroplasts** are found in some plant cells. They contain chlorophyll, a green substance which allows the plant to trap light energy from the Sun. You will find out more about this later.

The **vacuole** is a space filled with a liquid called cell sap.

In the activity, you will find out more about cells. You will need to use a microscope to see them.

Not all animal and plant cells look exactly like the cells on the right. Other cells are shown on the next page.

Cells from a human cheek, which have been stained and magnified about 200 times. The stain makes the cytoplasm appear green and the nuclei appear orange.

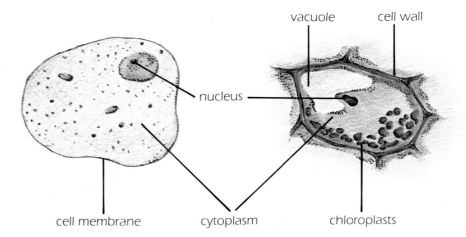

A human cheek cell   A pondweed cell

vacuole   cell wall

nucleus

cell membrane   cytoplasm   chloroplasts

**BODYWORKS**

will need to alter the focussing knob only slightly

■ Keep your slide.

■ Repeat with another piece of onion skin on a second slide, but use iodine stain instead of water.

■ Compare your two slides and make labelled drawings of what you see on each one. What did the iodine stain do?

■ Look at your own slides of onion cells or slide of a human cheek cell. How are plant cells similar to animal cells? How do plant cells differ from animal cells?

Plant leaf cells

A bundle of human muscle cells

A human nerve cell

1 Peeling off the skin

2 Laying the skin on a slide

## Looking at cells

■ Peel off a small piece of thin skin from the inside of your piece of onion. Hold the skin by its edge.

■ Lay the skin flat in the centre of a slide.

■ Add a drop of water.

■ Lower the cover slip on to the skin as shown in the diagram. Try to avoid trapping air bubbles.

■ Examine your slide under the low-power objective lens of the microscope.

■ Use a more powerful objective lens to have a closer look. You

3 Wetting the skin

4 Covering the skin

# Cells, tissues and organs

We have already seen that all living things are made up of cells. The cells of the human body are like the inhabitants of a country. We need people with different abilities, or specialists, who play different roles in the running of the country. We need people who can govern, fight disease, remove waste, provide our food and transport, and so on. In the same way, our bodies need cells with special abilities.

In the body there are special cells with particular jobs to do. Cells of the same type join together to form different types of **tissue**, each with their own special jobs. For example, muscle cells form the tissue in the wall of the stomach and the gut.

These tissues in turn are built up into larger units called **organs**, such as the heart, the lungs, the brain or the stomach.

## Organ systems

If you put some organs together to carry out an important process in your body, such as digestion, you have an **organ system**. The digestive system consists of the gullet, stomach, small and large intestine, rectum and anus.

All the organs and organ systems together make up an independent, living thing.

The organ systems carry out all the functions which are necessary for us to live.

You have already looked at some plant cells. Plant cells also make up tissues and organs which have special functions. You will find out more about these later in this course.

How many millions of cells do you think make up the body of this weightlifter?

# Bodybuilding

- Cut out the outline of the body on **data sheet D2.3**.
- Cut out the organs, organ systems, skull and rib-cage.
- Place the organs, organ systems, skull and rib-cage in the correct position on your body outline. You may need to use books to help you. Think before you glue. Some organs will need to go on top of others.
- What is the main function of the skull and rib-cage?
- Now stick the body you have made into your book.
- Label the main organs and organ systems.

Follow the plan

# What is health?

People seem to find it much easier to talk about their illnesses than about being in good health. Next time you are in a queue, listen to the grown-ups' conversations around you. If they are talking about health, they will probably be discussing what's wrong with them – their aches and pains.

This isn't because people are naturally miserable, or even because they are particularly unhealthy. It's because illness is much easier to talk about than healthiness. Being healthy means different things to different people. What do you mean by 'health' and 'being healthy'?

The next activity will help you to decide what being healthy really means.

## Have you got a healthy attitude?

Although we cannot control all the things that affect our health, there are many that we do have some control over.

- Think of all the things that might affect your health now and later in your lifetime.
- Divide these things into two lists under the headings:

*Things that I CAN control*
*Things that I CANNOT control*

Here is a list of features which could be used to describe a healthy person:
- is never ill
- does not drink alcohol
- gets up easily in the morning
- likes to play sports

THE MEDICINE WORKED A *TREAT,* I WAS UP AND ABOUT THE *NEXT* DAY! HOW'S YOUR FOOT, IS IT ANY *BETTER* ?

I'VE HAD THE 'FLU – THE WHOLE *FAMILY* HAS BEEN ILL, AND *NOW* BILLY'S ILL IN BED! HOW'S YOUR LOT ?

OH, MY BACK'S KILLING ME IT *MUST* HAVE BEEN TRYING TO SHIFT THAT FURNITURE YESTERDAY – IF IT GETS WORSE I'M OFF TO BED!

## How sweet!

You should know by now that too many sweet foods are bad for your teeth. Tiny living things, called **microorganisms,** which are in your mouth can breed very fast. They feed on the bits of food left on your teeth and they love sugar most of all.

If you do not clean your teeth, a sticky film called plaque builds up. It contains the sugar, the microorganisms and the acid they produce. This acid eats away the surface of teeth and tooth decay is the result.

■ List as many ways as you can to keep your teeth healthy.

Would you include any of these foods in a healthy diet?

41

# What happens to your food?

food

saliva

enzymes

stomach

## Breaking down the food

Saliva makes the food easier to swallow. It also contains a chemical substance called an **enzyme,** which turns starch from the food into sugar. Sugar and starch are both carbohydrates but sugar particles are smaller than starch particles.

enzymes

small intestine

food particles

You already know that all substances, including foods, are made of particles. Before your body can make use of the food you eat, the food must be broken down into these particles. We call this process **digestion**.

Digestion begins in the mouth. As we chew our food, it is broken into smaller pieces. A liquid called saliva is mixed with it. It is saliva which makes our mouths water when we think about something nice to eat!

Your digestive system is like this imaginary machine. Food enters the system at one end and passes along a tube where it is broken down or digested. There are three main sections: stomach, small intestine, large intestine

Nearly all digested food passes into the blood from the small intestine

**bloodstream**
Once the food is in the bloodstream, the blood takes it to the cells all over the body

used blood

kidneys remove waste liquid from blood

clean blood

42

The food travels on through the stomach and intestines. As it travels, more enzymes break down the carbohydrates, proteins and fats into smaller units. Eventually, the food particles are small enough to pass through the wall of the intestine into the bloodstream. The blood then takes the food to the cells all over the body.

Digestion means breaking food into particles small enough to enter the bloodstream.

Food that you cannot digest collects in the rectum and is passed out through the anus. In a healthy diet, much of this is fibre and is present in plant foods such as fruit and vegetables. It helps food move through the digestive system.

## The plastic gut

You are going to make a model of your intestines out of a piece of plastic tubing! In real life, your intestines would stretch for about 7 m if unravelled, but the tubing will act in some ways exactly like your intestines.

- Tie a knot at one end of the special plastic (visking) tubing.
- Open the other end and, using a dropper, half fill it with starch suspension.
- Add a few drops of enzyme solution.
- Tie a knot in the other end.
- Put the tubing into a boiling tube and almost fill the boiling tube with warm, distilled water.
- After 20 min, remove the plastic tubing.
- Divide the water in the visking tubing into two test-tubes.
- Test one for starch and the other for sugar. (Use **data sheet D2.5** to help you.)

- Record your observations.
- What has happened to the starch inside the tubing?
- Why is starch unable to enter the bloodstream?
- How do enzymes help digestion?

Record

large intestine

solid waste

rectum

liquid waste

The large intestine removes waste liquid from the undigested remains

anus

waste liquid

## Did you know?

Food stays in your stomach between one and a half and four hours. A meal takes about a day to travel right through you.

43

# How do plants get their food?

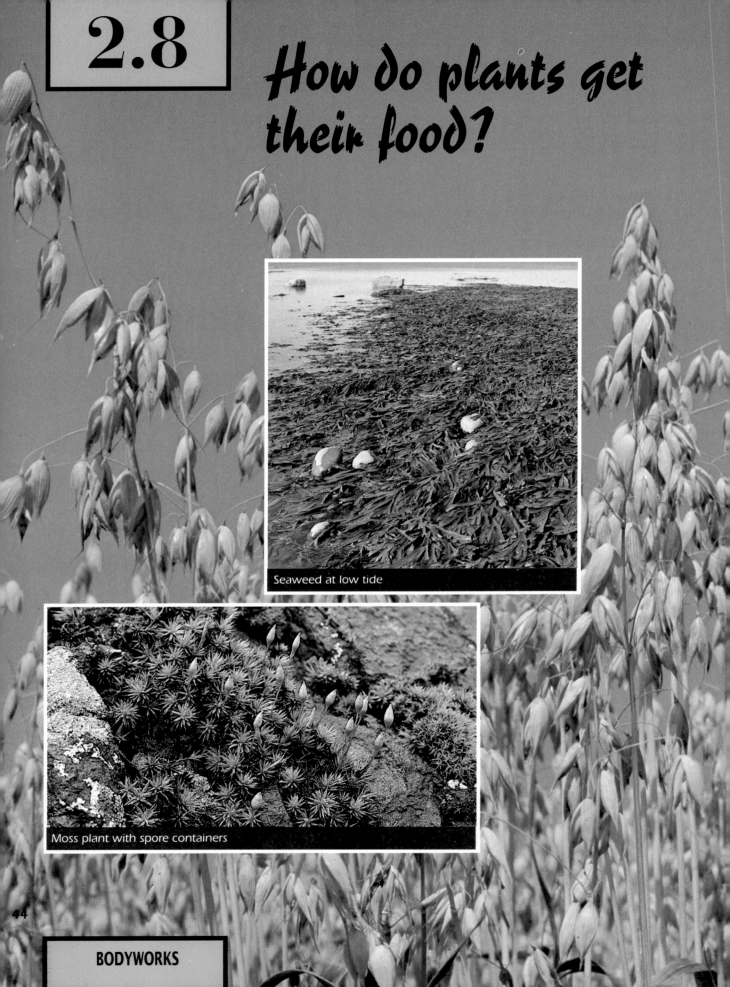

Seaweed at low tide

Moss plant with spore containers

BODYWORKS

Plants also need food to grow and produce energy, but they don't have a digestive system like yours.

So, how do plants get their food? You probably have some ideas about this already. In the next activity, you will be able to share your ideas with your friends and discuss your ideas as well as theirs.

You will then be able to test those ideas – scientists do this all the time.

## How does your garden grow?

■ Discuss with a group of friends how you think plants get their food.

■ Make a poster to illustrate your group's ideas.

■ With your teacher, list all the ideas which appear on your class posters.

■ Choose one of the ideas from the list and make an hypothesis which you can test.

■ To test your hypothesis, plan and carry out an investigation.using the 'exploration machine' at the front of this book to help you.

■ Produce another poster to illustrate your investigation.

■ Discuss with your friends whether your ideas are the same as they were before you carried out the exploration.

■ Compare your ideas with the information given on **data sheet D2.8.**

House plants: parlour palm (left) and ladder fern (right and back)

An oak tree in a spring meadow

# What happens to the air you breathe?

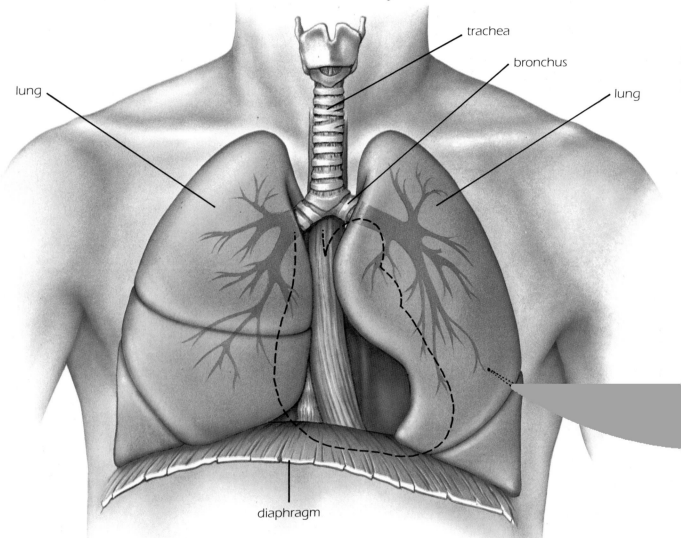

trachea

bronchus

lung

lung

diaphragm

You know that we need carbohydrates for energy, but we can only get this energy if we 'burn' carbohydrates by combining them with oxygen in our cells.

To get this oxygen, we need to breathe in air. When you breathe in, you increase the size of your chest by movements of your rib cage and a sheet of muscle below your ribs called the diaphragm.

## Respiration

Air enters your nose or mouth and passes down the windpipe, or trachea. Each lung is connected to the windpipe by a tube called a bronchus. Inside the lung, this tube divides many times. The smallest tubes end in a group of air sacs called alveoli. Blood flows around these air sacs. It collects oxygen from them, and carries it to all the cells of the body. Sugars from digested carbohydrates and the oxygen you breathe in meet in the cells. There they combine to produce energy to keep the body working.

The waste products of this reaction are the gases carbon dioxide and water vapour. These pass into the blood and are breathed out of the lungs. This whole process is called **respiration.**

Remember the respiration process, because you will need to write a word equation at the end of the next activity.

## Breathe in!

- Put your hands on your ribs and breathe in as deeply as you can. Which way do your ribs move?
- With a partner, measure the size of your chest after taking a deep breath and again after breathing out.

blood vessels

air sacs (alveoli)

When you breathe in, your ribs move outwards, causing air to be sucked into your lungs

When you breathe out, your ribs move inwards, causing air to be squeezed from your lungs

- Record your measurements in a table like this:

| Size of my chest after breathing in | |
|---|---|
| Size of my chest after breathing out | |

- How much bigger is your chest when you breathe in? The increase in chest size is called your chest expansion.

- Fill a 5 dm³ plastic container with water and then screw on the top.
- Turn the container upside down into a bowl of water.
- Remove the top under water and put one end of a rubber tube into the container.

- Take a deep breath and blow into the other end of the tube.
- Mark the new water level on the container.
- Empty the container completely, then measure how much water is needed to fill the container up to your mark. Use a 500 cm³ beaker for this.
- How much air can your lungs hold? We call this your lung capacity.
- Write the word equation for respiration, filling in the boxes with the words given.

Measure

**energy    sugar    oxygen
water vapour    carbon dioxide**

# Smoking

COLLECT YOUR COUPON BUTTS

BUTTS COLLECT YOUR COUPON FOR BRONCHITIS

BUTTS COLLECT YOUR COUPON FOR CANCER

LOW TO MIDDLE TAR

**Warning: SMOKING CAN CAUS**

Health Departmer

DON'T GET TO MIDDLE AGE AND SAY **BUTT** IF ONLY I HADN'T...

## Just say 'no'!

Have you ever been offered a cigarette? Write down where it was and who offered it to you. If not, think what you would do if you were offered a cigarette.

- Get into a group, with three or four friends.

- Your task is to act out a short sketch about smoking.
- Decide who will play these roles: a smoker; one or two very tempted non-smokers, one or two definite non-smokers.

You will have a 'quiet time' to study your role.

- Get your group together again. Decide upon your situation: in the school playground; on the bus home, for example.
- Each group will present their sketch to the class.
- Discuss these questions: In what ways are you encouraged to smoke? Should cigarette advertising be allowed? Do you think smoking should be banned in public places?

**BODYWORKS**

If someone asked you to breathe in a mixture of irritating, poisonous and cancer-causing substances, would you do it? Such substances are found in tobacco, so why do people smoke?

People start to smoke for all kinds of reasons. Young children may copy older brothers or sisters, teenagers may smoke because their friends do – they want to 'fit in' or appear 'grown-up'. Older people may have become smokers before the dangers were known. Now they are addicted to a drug called nicotine, present in tobacco. Nicotine is habit-forming and smokers' bodies and minds depend upon it.

Smoking gives you bad breath, stained teeth and dull, wrinkled skin. It causes coughs and chest infections. Cigarette smoke leaves a sticky deposit of tar in your lungs, which can cause cancer. Lung cancer kills more than 40 000 people every year in the UK and 90% of these are smokers.

*Passive smoking* means breathing in the smoke of other people's cigarettes.

The children of smokers get more lung illnesses than other children. Why is this?

efined by H.M. Government

# UNG CANCER & HEART DISEASE
hief Medical Officers

dull, wrinkled skin

bad breath, stained teeth

throat cancer

chest infections, lung cancer

heart disease

## Did you know?

In Britain, 100 000 people die every year as a direct result of smoking.

# Blood circulation: the transport system

You know that your cells need food and oxygen which are carried in your blood. How does the blood get round your body?

## First circuit

Blood is pumped round the body by the heart. The heart beats between 45 and 70 times a minute. The blood leaves the heart through tubes called **arteries** which take the blood to all parts of the body. The arteries divide into tiny tubes called **capillaries** which pass through your tissues and take food and oxygen to the cells.

The blood travels back to the heart, first in capillaries and then in larger vessels called **veins.**

## Second circuit

The blood then begins a second circuit – through the lungs. In the lungs, the waste carbon dioxide leaves the blood and is breathed out. The red blood cells collect fresh oxygen. The blood returns to the heart ready for another circuit round the body.

Heart disease in adults usually occurs because arteries get clogged up with a fatty substance from the blood. If one of the arteries supplying the heart with blood becomes completely blocked, the person will have a heart attack. In Britain, heart disease kills more people than any other illness.

■ Look back at the activity on spread 2.5.
■ Discuss how you can keep your heart healthy.

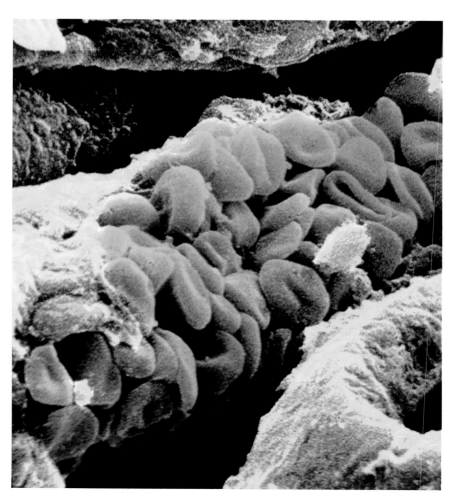

Red blood cells (magnified 600 times) in a capillary. The photograph is coloured so that the blood cells appear red and the capillary walls appear green

**William Harvey 1578–1657**
In 1625, Harvey discovered that blood circulated round the body. Before that, people thought that blood passed back and forth in two separate parts of the body.
■ Find out more about Harvey's discovery, his life and the times in which he lived.

## Did you know?

● Your heart beats about 100 000 times a day.
● It takes 60 s for blood to make a complete circuit round your body.
● There are about 100 000 km of blood vessels in your body.

**BODYWORKS**

Feel the pulse in a friend's wrist using the tip of your middle finger. What is his or her pulse rate?

- Now do 2 min vigorous exercise. Your teacher may make some suggestions.
- Measure your pulse rate straight away after the exercise.
- Keep measuring your pulse rate for 1 min every 2 min until it returns to normal.
- Devise a way to record your results. Draw a line graph to show your pulse rate before and after exercise.

Your blood vessels are like a system of pipes. The heart pumps blood to the body tissues, and then it returns to the lungs

## Finger on the pulse

- Hold one hand out palm upwards.
- Place the tip of the middle finger of your other hand on your wrist, as shown in the photograph.
- When you have found your pulse, count the number of beats in 1 min. This is your pulse rate.
- Repeat this twice and record all three figures.

- Find the average pulse rate. Add the three figures and divide by three.

|  | Pulse rate |
|---|---|
| 1 |  |
| 2 |  |
| 3 |  |
| Total |  |
| Average pulse rate (total ÷ 3) |  |

- How long did it take for your pulse rate to return to normal (the average pulse rate worked out at the beginning)? People who take a lot of exercise and are fit recover quickly. Their pulse rate returns to normal more rapidly than those who are less fit.

  It may be interesting to compare your recovery rate with others in your class.

51

# How your body moves

The human skeleton is built up of more than 200 bones which support and protect the body organs from injury. The bones also provide a solid base for the muscles to work against.

The bones of the skeleton meet at many joints. Some are fixed joints, allowing no movement. Other joints allow us to move in various ways. **Data sheet D2.12** shows four types of joint and how they work.

## Muscle control

Movements occur when we contract muscles. Muscles are a special type of tissue which is elastic. There are two main types. Involuntary muscles are normally controlled by the brain with no continuous effort. The muscles involved in breathing and heart beating are of this type. Voluntary muscles are those which we are able to control at will.

*A human skeleton*

arm flexed

arm extended

To bend your arm, the large muscle at the top, called the biceps, shortens. The muscle under the arm lengthens

## Movement and me

- Work with a partner for this activity.
- Copy this table into your book.
- Either you or your partner should try to keep absolutely still for 5 min.
- The other one should watch carefully and record any movement, no matter how small, in the table.

- Swop over and repeat the activity.
- Discuss with your partner what sorts of movements each of you made during the activity. Were they voluntary or involuntary?

Record

| What moved | Description of movement e.g. up, down, turn, etc. | Movement group | What useful job the movement does |
|---|---|---|---|
|  |  |  |  |

## Move those bones!

You are going to examine three different types of joint movements in your own skeleton.

- Type **A** joints allow movement in one direction (or plane) only – like the hinge on a cupboard door.
- Type **B** joints allow movement in two different directions.
- Type **C** joints allow sliding movement.

Use **data sheet D2.12** to help you.

- Devise a way to record all the different movements that your skeleton can make.
- Sort all the movements into types **A**, **B**, **C**.
- Choose a way to present all this information so that you can show how many of the different types of movement there are in your body.

# How fit are you?

Exercise helps make your body healthy, fit and strong.

When you exercise, your heart beats faster, your breathing is faster and you feel tired but, the fitter you are, the quicker you will recover.

## Strength and stamina

Muscles will waste away if they are not used, but regular exercise will build them up, increasing their size and strength. Exercise increases the stamina of muscles. This means that they get used to physical effort and do not tire quickly after a short burst of activity.

## Suppleness and general health

If joints are not stretched regularly, they will become stiff. Exercise keeps them supple. Regular exercise improves your appetite, helps digestion and

reduces your chances of future heart diseases. Exercise helps to keep you fit.

A low pulse rate is a sign of fitness. Unfit people with high pulse rates should not suddenly take vigorous exercise. They should follow a sensible programme of exercise and increase their fitness over a period of time.

Swimming is a good, all-round exercise

## Exploration: Get moving!

Julie staggered over the finish line at the end of the cross-country race.

'Well done, Julie!' said her teacher, Mr Holloway. 'That's a personal best time. How do you feel now?'

Julie couldn't answer. She was panting for breath and her pulse was racing. It was a cold day, but she felt hot and sweaty.

■ Plan and carry out an exploration to discover the effects of various types of exercise.

**Remember:**
- Follow the 'exploration machine'.
- Report your exploration under the headings:
*Task, Plan, Action, Interpretation.*

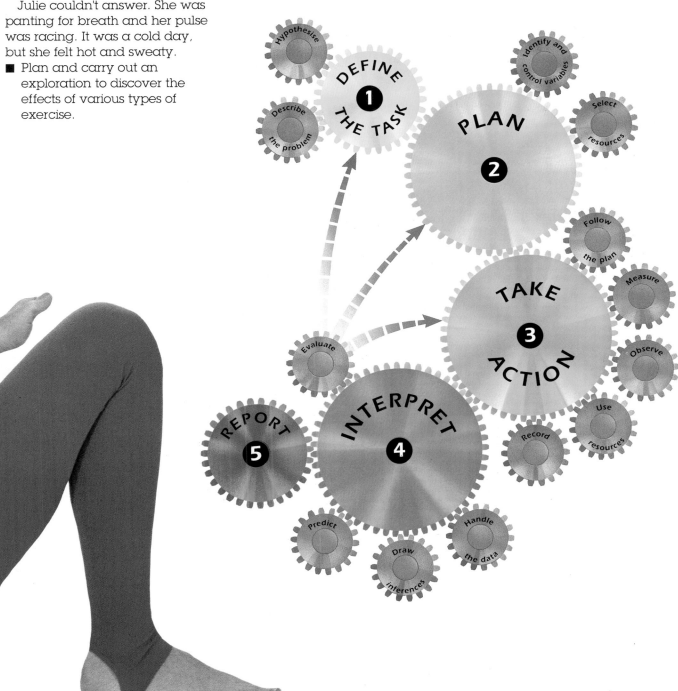

Hypothesise

Describe the problem

**DEFINE THE TASK** ❶

Identify and control variables

Select resources

**PLAN** ❷

Follow the plan

Measure

Observe

**TAKE ACTION** ❸

Evaluate

Use resources

Record

**REPORT** ❺

**INTERPRET** ❹

Predict

Draw inferences

Handle the data

55

# Message received

Our bodies are receiving messages from our surroundings all the time. What messages are you receiving now? How does your body interpret them? How do you react to them?

Your central nervous system consists of the brain, the spinal cord and the nerves.

Your brain controls all your activities. You do not even have to think about some of them, like breathing or blinking for example! The brain also receives messages from your eyes, ears and other sense organs.

## Sending signals

Your spinal cord is an extension of your brain. From it, nerves branch off to reach all parts of your body.

Your brain reacts to messages received by sending signals back to the muscles. Different parts of the brain receive different types of message. You react so quickly that sometimes you don't have time to think. What would happen if you picked up a hot test-tube by mistake? This type of reaction is called a reflex action.

Voluntary actions are actions over which you have control.
■ Are the following actions reflex or voluntary: blinking; laughing; picking up a pencil; sneezing; scratching?

*Your brain is like a computer. It receives messages carried along nerves in your body and spinal cord. Information from your eyes, ears and nose is also sent to your brain for processing*

# How do you react?

How quickly do you think your nerves send messages to your brain and back again to your muscles? The time taken is your reaction time.

- Work in pairs. Your partner will hold a metre rule vertically so that the end (zero mark) is between your first finger and thumb. The ruler must not touch your finger or thumb.
- Look at the zero mark on the ruler – your partner will drop it when you are not expecting it! You must not look at him or her for clues.
- When the ruler is dropped, catch it as quickly as you can.
- Make a note of the distance the ruler drops. Use the graph on **data sheet D2.14** to change the distance into a time. What is this time?
- Repeat this five times and work out an average.
- Change partners and repeat the experiment.

- Can you think of ways of reducing the time taken to catch the ruler?
- Try any ideas you have for shortening the time.
- Do you think that tiredness may affect your reaction time? How?
- Make an hypothesis about the effect of tiredness on your reaction time.
- Plan and carry out an investigation to test your hypothesis.

Adult human brain

# Behaving badly

A habit is something we do regularly. Some habits are healthy and safe, for example cleaning our teeth or looking both ways before crossing the road. Other habits are bad for us; some may be deadly. A habit that is difficult to give up is called addiction.

People can be addicted to a variety of substances. Smoking, drinking alcohol, taking drugs and sniffing glue or solvents are all addictive. Any of these substances can damage your body and affect your mind.

## Alcohol abuse

Having a drink seems to be very adult, yet alcohol can cause great damage to people and their families. Many road accidents are due to people who have drunk too much. When you drink too much it is difficult to judge speed and distance – both vital if you are to drive safely. Alcohol can make people lose their self-control and do things that they would never do if they were sober. Many fights start because people drink too much.

*In the UK, over one million people are drinking alcohol at levels which will seriously damage their health*

Many young people have died from sniffing substances like glue and aerosols.

■ Discuss with your friends why people sniff glue, use drugs or drink alcohol.
■ Do you think you can 'just try it once and get away with it?'

**BODYWORKS**

## Harmful habits

### Part 1

- On **data sheet D2.15,** choose five of the influences listed and then fill in the boxes.
- Check and discuss your decisions with a partner.

### Part 2

We come across solvents every day. What is a solvent?

Most solvents are harmless, but some give off vapours (gases) which can be harmful. When you sniff these vapours, they pass into your lungs and then into your blood. What might happen next?

- Read the passage above from the *Daily Horizon*.

# 11 YEAR OLD GIRL DIES AFTER GLUE-SNIFFING

An 11 year old girl died today after experimenting with glue-sniffing for the first time. The girl, named only as Lynda, was at a party with a group of friends at the time of her death. One of the group told police that Lynda had been called 'chicken' because she would not join in the glue-sniffing at first. Eventually, she was persuaded to. She passed out and vomited. She then choked to death on her own sick.

- Draw a storyboard similar to those you have seen in magazines. Make a series of about six drawings which illustrate the story of Lynda and her friends. Give not only their words, but also their thoughts.
- Consider these two points and include them in your storyboard – they may alter the ending of the story:
  How could Lynda's friends have helped her?
  What is meant by 'peer group pressure'? How can this influence the decisions that people make?

59

# Defend yourself!

Microorganisms are so small that we can only see them by using a powerful microscope. Many of them are useful in the production of foods like cheese and yogurt. Some microorganisms can cause disease and these are often called 'germs'.

## Bacteria

**Bacteria** are microorganisms consisting of a single cell. Many live in our bodies and cause us no harm. Others can make us very ill if they enter the body. Microorganisms which cause disease are called **pathogens**. Sore throats, stomach upsets and more serious diseases like typhoid and tuberculosis are caused by bacteria. Bacteria reproduce by dividing in two, this can happen every 20 min. So large numbers of bacteria are produced quickly.

## Viruses

**Viruses** are even smaller than bacteria. One million could fit into a single bacterium! An especially powerful microscope called an electron microscope is needed to see a virus. Viruses may cause diseases in plants and animals. The common cold, influenza, measles, and AIDS are all caused by viruses.

Bacteria like these exist in the nose and throat and on the skin of healthy people

## Your defence force

When microorganisms enter your body, white blood cells are produced. These are your body's defence force. Some white cells eat pathogens and destroy them. Others produce chemicals called antibodies which destroy the pathogens. When antibodies are produced to fight one particular disease, they may remain in

A photograph from an electron microscope coloured to show a white blood cell engulfing a foreign cell. This process is called phagocytosis and is part of the body's defence system

Some types of bacteria

Staphylococcus
(can cause boils)

Streptococcus
(can cause sore throats)

rod-shaped bacillus
(some can cause diseases)

your body and protect you from that disease in the future. You are then said to be immune to that disease.

Doctors can immunise people against some diseases. They give the patient a vaccine containing weak or dead microorganisms which cause a particular disease. By producing the right antibodies, your body is prepared to fight that disease in the future. Which diseases have you been immunised against?

Diseases that are passed from person to person are called infectious. You may have heard people say that a 'bug' is going around. What does this mean?

■ Carry out a survey of the infectious diseases that members of your class have had. Choose a good way to record and display the results of your survey.

## Did you know?

The smallest independently-living thing is a bacterium living in sewage. Ten thousand of these bacteria side by side would measure only 1 mm.

## What's bugging you?

If you have ever had influenza or 'flu, chickenpox or any other infectious disease, you may remember that your body temperature was high. This is one of the symptoms of fever and is a sign that your body is fighting the disease.

■ Look at the graph of body temperature and illness.
■ Copy it into your book. Write the words 'fever', 'recovery', and 'infection' in the correct place on the graph.

**Body temperature and illness**

Temperature (°C)

41 —
40 —
39 —
38 —
37 —

Days

# Keeping food fresh

Microorganisms are all around us. They may travel in air currents and if they land on uncovered food they may multiply and cause the food to go bad.

Many of these microorganisms will make the food smell, taste or look unpleasant. Other bacteria that contaminate food are very dangerous, but may not give us the warnings of a nasty smell or a bad taste.

Other microorganisms can cause food poisoning if the contaminated food is eaten. Salmonella is a bacterium which, if eaten in large numbers, will cause fever symptoms, diarrhoea and sickness. The Salmonella bacterium is killed by heat.

Food lasts longer if it is kept cold. Refrigeration slows down the rate at which bacteria multiply, so they cannot break food down quickly.

- Here are some statements about safe cooking. Why are they true?
- Pre-prepared food should always be cooked at a temperature of over 100°C.
- Food should not be kept warm for a long period of time.
- Frozen chickens should always be completely thawed before cooking.

Some foods are heat-treated so that they keep longer. What does the heating do?

## Gone off!

Reazurin is a blue dye which changes colour in sour milk.

- Label your test-tubes A, B, C.
- Put 10 cm³ of fresh pasteurised milk into A.
- Put 10 cm³ of 2 day old pasteurised milk into B.
- Put 10 cm³ of 4 day old pasteurised milk into C.
- Put 1 cm³ of Reazurin into each test-tube.
- Cork the tubes and shake them well.
- Put the tubes into a beaker of warm water (about 45°C).
- Observe and record any colour changes in a table like the one below.
- How fresh is each sample?
- Bacteria make the milk go off. How do you think the bacteria get into the milk?
- What does the test tell you about the number of bacteria in each sample?
- In what ways could you keep milk fresh for as long as possible?
- Why do you think you were told to use 10 cm³ each time?

| Colour after ... minutes | Milk samples | | |
|---|---|---|---|
| | A | B | C |
| 0 | | | |
| 1 | | | |
| 5 | | | |
| 10 | | | |
| 20 | | | |
| 30 | | | |

# Weather affects us all

## Weatherwatch

**Meteorology** is a branch of science which studies the weather. Meteorologists use the scientific method. They observe and measure the weather. They look for patterns, explain the patterns and then make predictions about the weather to come. You are going to find out how meteorologists work and how important the weather is to us all.

How often do you hear people complain about the weather? One day you are 'drenched', the next you 'freeze' – or 'bake'.

The weather can be good:

> 'BANK HOLIDAY RUSH TO THE BEACHES AS THE NATION SWELTERS IN THE SUN.'

The weather can be treacherous:

> 'TROPICAL CYCLONE STRIKES BANGLADESH. THOUSANDS MADE HOMELESS. SATELLITE PICTURES WARNED OF STORM.'

The weather can be devastating:

> 'INSURANCE COMPANIES PAY OUT MILLIONS AFTER THE GREAT STORM.'

Storms can destroy in seconds trees which have taken many years to grow

Tropical flooding makes life difficult for cyclists

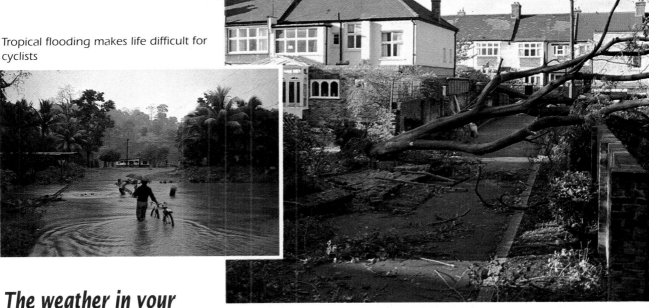

## The weather in your community

**You, your family and friends**

- Make a list of the outdoor activities you have taken part in over the last week or so.
- Beside each activity, describe how the weather could affect it. Also include activities your family or friends take part in. Examples could include playing netball, fishing, gardening, trips to the seaside, taking your dog for a walk, going to the shops, etc.

| Activity | Effects of the weather |
|---|---|
|  |  |

| Local services and industries | Effects of the weather |
|---|---|
| Building | |
| Farming | |
| Transport | |
| Traffic police | |
| Leisure centres | |
| Tourism | |
| Clothing manufacturers | |

**Your community**

- Think about how the weather affects local services and industries. Some people can make money because of the weather, others can lose money because of it.
- Copy and complete the table shown below.
- Write down how the weather might affect how much money they make.

# Climate and agriculture

Farming depends on the climate more than most other industries. Just a few weeks without rain or a late frost in spring can set back a crop, and that means higher prices in the shops.

Agricultural scientists test the effects of high rainfall, of high **humidity,** of low temperatures and other conditions crops might have to go through.
- Why do you think this scientific research is so valuable?

Now, plan your way through the gardening year.
- Collect **data sheet D3.2**. Use it to decide when to cultivate the soil and when to start the crops off.

## Farmers are always complaining!

| | |
|---|---|
| Too much rain | Soil becomes too wet and unworkable. Soil can be compacted by farm vehicles. |
| Too little rain | Soil dries out. Costly irrigation needed. |
| Too hot | Some pests and plant diseases thrive. |
| Too cold | Plants grow slowly. Poor yields. |
| Too windy | Crops flattened. Livestock affected by chilly winds. |

**WEATHERWATCH**

# Grow a crop

Broad beans are an easy crop to grow, and are quite tolerant of weather conditions. One variety is called *Aquadulce claudia*. It can be sown outdoors from late October to December. The young plants will survive most winters, but in cold spells, cloches should be used for protection.

- Suggest some ways a cloche can protect a young plant. Suggest an advantage of growing a crop which overwinters.
- Collect five jam jars and label them A, B, C, D and E. Collect some blotting paper and cut it to line the insides of the jars.
- Collect some broad bean seeds and place them between the blotting paper and the walls of the jars, as shown in the diagram.
- To jars A, B and C, add water to a depth of 1 cm.
- Completely fill jar D with water, but leave jar E dry.
- Leave jars A, D and E in the laboratory.
- Place jar B in the refrigerator.
- Place jar C in an incubator set between 35°C and 40°C.
- Record your observations over the next two weeks, in a table like the one below.

A cloche, or glass tent, to protect tender plants

blotting paper          broad bean

- It may be necessary to top-up the water level during the investigation. Why do you think you may need to do this?
- Compare your results with others in the class. Record what you have found out about growing a crop in different conditions.
- Scientists studying plants have to replicate (repeat) their experiments. Why do you think this is?

| Jar | Simulated weather conditions | Observations |
|-----|------------------------------|--------------|
| A | Ideal conditions | |
| B | Frost | |
| C | Heat | |
| D | Flood | |
| E | Drought | |

# Watching the weather worldwide

There are thousands of weather stations throughout the world that measure and record every possible aspect of the weather. Many stations are fully automatic. Their work is overseen by the World Meteorological Organisation (WMO) which is based in Geneva, Switzerland.

The weather stations include ships which release special balloons with radios to provide information about conditions at altitudes up to 30 km. Aircraft transmit data to ground stations and, since 1960, there have been weather **satellites** in orbit above the Earth.

Weather satellites transmit pictures which show the clouds above the Earth, and other weather data, including temperature.

A weather satellite and ground receiving station

**WEATHERWATCH**

- Have you seen any weather satellite pictures on television? Here is a list of different measurements that weather stations can make.
  - temperature
  - rainfall
  - snow
  - hail
  - dew
  - visibility
  - air pressure
  - humidity
  - cloud cover
  - thunder
  - lightning
- Can you suggest any more?
- Why are all these measurements useful?

A METEOSAT image of western Europe. Can you identify the best place to be when this photograph was taken?

# Weather satellites

There are two main types of weather satellite.

*Polar orbiting satellites*
These orbit the Earth in 100 min at an altitude of about 1000 km. They are able to photograph the entire Earth's surface over a period of time.

*Geostationary satellites*
These are positioned at a height of 36 000 km above the equator and orbit with the Earth. Thus, they never move from their spot over the equator. They can only photograph one side of the Earth, but the pictures can be transmitted non-stop.
- Why do geostationary satellites usually give poor pictures of the polar regions?
- Try to find out about geostationary satellites and the scientists involved in their development. Arthur C. Clarke, a science fiction author, was a pioneer in satellite development.

These pictures show the orbits of the two types of satellite. Can you work out which is which?

METEOSAT is a weather satellite receiver and the European Space Agency operates the METEOSAT transmissions.
- What information can we obtain from METEOSAT?

# Temperature

Temperature is a measure of how hot or cold things are. We measure temperature using a thermometer.

## Thermometers

There are several different types of thermometer.

*Electronic temperature sensors*
These can record the temperature continually for several days. A computer can then display the information on a television screen.

*Glass tubes filled with mercury or dyed alcohol*
These liquids expand or swell when they warm up and shrink when they cool down.

*Electronic maximum and minimum thermometers*
These can give outdoor and indoor temperatures simultaneously on twin digital displays. Maximum and minimum buttons enable the user to read the highest and lowest temperatures recorded both outside and inside. Maximum and minimum thermometers can also be made from glass tubes filled with mercury.

*Clinical thermometers*
These have a narrow range for measuring body temperature. You may have used one to take your temperature when you are ill.

### The Celsius scale
Scientists use the Celsius scale for measuring temperature. This scale is named after the Swedish astronomer Anders Celsius (1701–44) and used to be called the 'centigrade scale', but in 1948, scientists agreed to rename the scale after its inventor. On the Celsius scale, the temperature of freezing water is 0, and the boiling point of water is 100.

*This mini weather station automatically measures temperature by means of an electronic sensor. Its other sensors measure different aspects of the weather*

Meteorologists all over the world must measure temperature under the same conditions. So, whether in the heat of Arabia or the cold of Sweden, they put their thermometers in well-ventilated boxes with slatted sides. These are called **Stevenson screens**. The screens keep the thermometers in the shade and protect them from the rain, while allowing air to circulate freely.
- What is temperature a measure of?
- Why should thermometers be placed in Stevenson screens?

## Measuring temperature

You can use either electronic temperature sensors or mercury-in-glass thermometers for these investigations.
- Check the accuracy of your thermometer by placing it in icy water, then in boiling pure water. What temperature would you expect it to show in these conditions?
- Find out what room temperature is. Does temperature vary in the room? Where is the best place to measure it? What are you measuring the temperature of?

*Measure*

### Did you know?
- The lowest natural temperature ever recorded on Earth, −89.2°C, occurred at Vostok, Antarctica, on 21 July 1983.
- The highest natural temperature recorded is 58°C at Al'Aziziyah, Libya, on 13 September 1922.

- What is the air temperature outside? Is there a difference between shade and direct sunlight? Is there a difference between measurements near buildings or far away from them? Is there a difference near north-facing walls or south-facing walls? Is there a difference high up or at ground level?

- Is there a pattern linking room temperature and the outside temperature? Find out when the central heating is switched on and off. What does this depend on? Are some parts of the school warmer than others? If so, try to explain the reason why.

- Use maximum and minimum thermometers for several days. How do they work?

- Arrange to get continuous temperature readings over a 24-hour period. Use a computer to plot the data as a graph. Explain the shape of the graph.

A computer can be used to record temperatures and show changes on the screen

Automatic weather stations like the one being set up below, are used to record basic weather data in remote areas

# Rainfall

Rain isn't just rain! Meteorologists have identified several different types of rainfall:
- drizzle (very small droplets that fall slowly)
- light rain
- heavy rain
- cloudburst (large droplets that fall very quickly)

and if it's cold enough, hail, sleet and snow.

However it falls, it is called **precipitation.**

The way in which rain falls is important. If too much falls too quickly, flooding could result. Heavy rain does not soak into the ground, it just runs off. Valuable topsoil can be washed away.

If too little rain falls, droughts occur and artificial watering or irrigation is needed. Countries like Pakistan, Israel and parts of the USSR all depend on irrigation for their cereal and fruit crops.

## Rain gauges and radar

Rainfall is collected in rain gauges. These measure the depth of water that would lie on the ground, evaporate or soak into the soil. Rainfall is measured in millimetres, and annual figures range from over 11 000 mm in Hawaii to less than 1 mm in parts of Chile.

Electronic rain gauges can record rainfall daily or over a

## Measuring rainfall

- Make a rain gauge using a plastic bottle as shown in the picture below.
- Measure the daily rainfall over the next few weeks using your rain gauge.
- Plot a graph of your data.
- Collect one 100 cm³ beaker and one 250 cm³ beaker. Place them side by side and pour water into them both at the same time using a watering can with a fine rose. Measure the height of water in each beaker. Explain your observations.
- It is possible that some rain water will evaporate from your rain gauge. What might this do to the reading?

Investigate this as follows.
- Collect two 250 cm³ beakers and half fill them with water to exactly the same level. Carefully pour a very thin layer of oil over the water in one beaker. Leave them for a few days and compare the loss of water by evaporation. Explain your results.
- What is the best location for your rain gauge? Does it matter if it is near buildings or trees?
- Measure the pH of rain using universal indicator paper. Is the rain you collected acidic, neutral or alkaline?

### Did you know?

- The wettest place on Earth is Tutunendo, Columbia, which has 11 770 mm of rainfall each year.
- Over 1870 mm of rain fell on Cilaos, La Réunion, in the Indian Ocean, during a 24-hour period on 15–16 March 1952 – the most intensive burst of rainfall ever recorded.

longer period. They can be plugged into computer systems for the display of data. They also empty themselves automatically.

Meteorologists use radar to detect rain. Radar can give 15 min warnings of rain before it actually arrives.

Old-style rain gauges consist of an outer case and funnel made from copper with a can inside to catch the rain.

# Wind speed and direction

Wind is moving air. It can blow in any direction, including up and down. Upward moving air in large storm clouds can be strong enough to destroy aircraft. Wind speed is usually measured in metres per second, knots or miles per hour by **anemometers**. However, anyone can find out the wind speed using the **Beaufort scale**.

## When the wind blows

Wind direction is given as where the wind has come from. A north wind comes from the north and goes to the south. Wind vanes and weather cocks are designed so that they point to where the wind has come from.

In a south-westerly wind, where will a weather cock point? Why does the shape of the weather cock make it point this way? Meteorologists record wind direction in degrees from 0°(north) to 90°(east) to 180°(south) to 270°(west) and back to north.

| Description | calm | light air | light breeze | gentle breeze | moderate breeze | fresh breeze |  |
|---|---|---|---|---|---|---|---|
| Effects on land | smoke rises vertically | smoke drifts a little, but not flags | leaves rustle, wind felt on face | leaves and twigs move, flags extended | paper and dust raised, small branches move | small trees sway | |
| Beaufort scale | 0 | 1 | 2 | 3 | 4 | 5 | |
| Wind speed | below 1 mph | 1–3 mph | 4–7 mph | 8–12 mph | 13–18 mph | 19–24 mph | |

**WEATHERWATCH**

The British Isles have very changeable weather. This is because several air flows meet here. Air which comes from the Atlantic Ocean carries more water vapour and is usually warmer. Dry air from central Europe is hot in summer and cold in winter.

- Look at the diagram below. What sort of weather would a northerly wind bring?

## Wind measurements

### Wind speed
- Design and make a flap anemometer. You will need **data sheet D3.6a.**
- Calibrate your flap anemometer using the Beaufort scale as a guide.
- Investigate wind speed in different locations around your school.

A cup anemometer for measuring wind speed

### Wind direction
- Design and make a wind vane. Use the information on **data sheet D3.6a.**
- Investigate wind direction in different locations around your school.

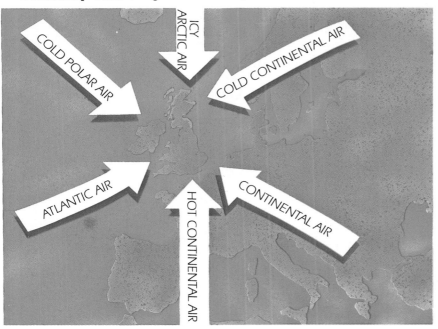

ICY ARCTIC AIR

COLD POLAR AIR

COLD CONTINENTAL AIR

ATLANTIC AIR

HOT CONTINENTAL AIR

CONTINENTAL AIR

Record

## Did you know?

The highest wind speed ever recorded is 450 km/h during a tornado at Wichita Falls, Texas, USA, on 2 April 1958.

| strong breeze | near gale | gale | strong gale | storm | violent storm | hurricane |
|---|---|---|---|---|---|---|
| large branches sway, umbrellas hard to use | trees sway, hard to walk against wind | twigs broken off, very hard to walk | minor damage to houses and roofs | trees uprooted, serious house damage | widespread damage | disaster, severe damage |
| 6 | 7 | 8 | 9 | 10 | 11 | 12 |
| 25–31 mph | 32–38 mph | 39–46 mph | 47–54 mph | 55–63 mph | 64–72 mph | above 72 mph |

# Forecasting the weather

The annual growth rings of felled trees can reveal climate changes over years. Wet years produce wide rings; drier years produce thinner rings

The work of meteorologists is more than simply taking measurements. They must also understand and be able to explain the measurements if they are to use them to make forecasts that are accurate.

Forecasting is needed for the short-term, to help farmers, builders, pilots, and others. However, forecasting for the long-term future could be much more important.

Would we know about gradual changes in climate if we did not have temperature readings from the past?

## Global climate change

Scientists have begun to think carefully about global climate change. Average global temperatures have risen over the last hundred years. This has caused sea levels to rise. Sea

TODAYS WEATHER

- Start your own record of weather observations.
- Draw up a table to record your weather observations. Here is a list of variables that you can observe:
  - cloud data
  - rainfall
  - wind speed
  - wind direction
  - temperature.

    Add any more you think of.
- You could also include columns with headings such as the examples below:

  *The weather now*

  *My forecast for tomorrow*

  *How the weather affected what I did today*

- Decide the following: how often you will make recordings; at what time you will make recordings; for how long you are going to make recordings.
- Make your first set of observations.
- When you have finished recording your observations, write a summary of how the weather changed.
- Were there any patterns to your records? Did, for example, cool showery weather follow mild rainy weather or did fog follow clear skies and sunny weather?
- How would you make use of these patterns to forecast (predict) the weather?

levels could rise by 30 cm over the next 40 years, due partly to melting glaciers, partly to melting ice at the poles, and partly to the oceans swelling up because they would be warmer.

There could be flooding on a large scale. Some low-lying islands would disappear. People would be forced to move because either their homes or their farm land would become submerged under seawater.

As the climate changes, so the pattern of agriculture would change. The British Isles may be better suited to crops like maize or sunflowers, rather than cereals. There may be changes to ocean currents, affecting the distribution of fish.

## The greenhouse effect

Scientists have shown that global warming is caused by an increase in certain gases in the atmosphere, mainly from burning coal, oil, petrol and other fuels. These gases cause the atmosphere to trap energy like a greenhouse. The heating produced is called the greenhouse effect.

Draw inferences

What do you think is the link between this photograph and the greenhouse effect?

77

# It's raining, it's pouring

Rainfall has caused this mud slide

When rain falls, it either soaks into the soil, or it runs off taking the top layer of soil with it. What happens depends on the size of the raindrops.

If too much topsoil is washed away it causes several problems:
- shallow soil
- poorer quality soil
- blocked drains
- rivers full of solids.

Identify and control variables

Select resources

Hypothesise

Describe the problem

**DEFINE THE TASK 1**

**PLAN 2**

78

## Exploration: Raindrop size and soil run-off

- Plan and carry out an exploration into how raindrop size affects the amount of soil washed away.
- Use the 'exploration machine' to help you.
- Use sand instead of soil for your exploration.
- Which type of rainfall is best suited to farmland?

- How could farmers minimise any damage caused to their land by rainfall?
- Can you think of any advantages to cloudburst rainfall?
- Apart from agriculture, what else might be affected by the different types of rain?

**Remember:**
- Follow the 'exploration machine'.
- Report your exploration under the headings:
*Task, Plan, Action, Interpretation.*

# Where is it hottest?

The Sun is 150 000 000 km from the Earth! The Sun produces very large amounts of energy. However, because it is so far away, only a small amount of its energy reaches the Earth.

The Earth is continually moving around the Sun. It takes one year to travel around the Sun, and it spins on its own axis at the same time. The axis of the Earth's spin is tilted at 23° from the vertical.

Different parts of the Earth may be hot or cold. It depends on how much of the Sun's radiated energy reaches the Earth's surface. For example, clouds reflect some of the Sun's light and warmth and stop it reaching the Earth's surface.

The tilt of the Earth also has an effect. You will investigate this in the following activity shown on the opposite page.

The Sun's rays are more concentrated near the equator than elsewhere. Can you see why? Do the rays pass through more atmosphere near the equator or near the North Pole? What effect does this have?

area of beam near the North Pole

area of beam near the equator

**WEATHERWATCH**

# Moving round the Sun

- Use a round object (e.g. a polystyrene sphere) to represent the Earth.
- Mark on the North and South Poles. You could use pins or coloured sticky labels.
- Mark on the equator, the Tropic of Cancer, and the Tropic of Capricorn. (Ask your teacher if you need help.)
- Tilt your model Earth as shown. The Earth is always tilted like this as it travels around the Sun.
- Shine a light on your model Earth. This represents sunlight. Keep the Earth tilted.
- Slowly move your model Earth one complete turn around the Sun, rotating the Earth at the same time. Always keep the North Pole pointing in exactly the same direction and keep the Earth at the same level as the Sun.

North Pole

Tropic of Cancer

equator

Tropic of Capricorn

South Pole

angle of tilt of the Earth

- As you move the Earth, write down which part of it is directly opposite the Sun (e.g. the northern hemisphere, the southern hemisphere or the equator).
- Mark where you live on the Earth with a coloured label.
- Again, move your model Earth around the Sun. Write down when it will be coldest for your country, and when it will be warmest. Why?
- Why do we have seasons? How do the seasons differ in Australia and on the equator?
- Why does day length change at different times of the year?
- Why do we have day and night on Earth?

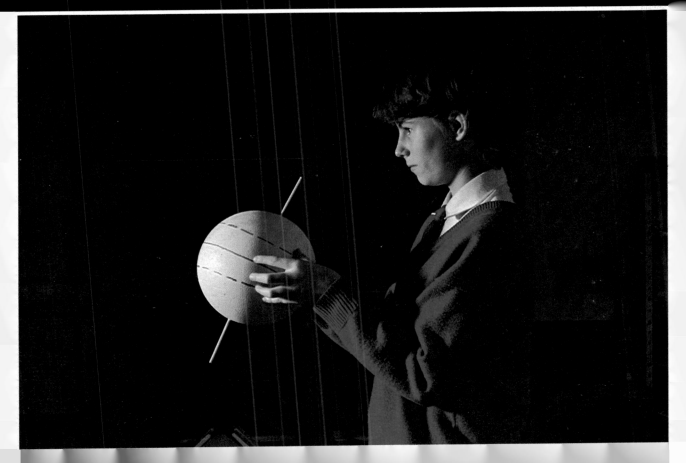

# Heat makes wind

Here are three investigations to help you understand how heat makes wind. You should do all three investigations.

## Investigation A

- Sellotape a heatproof mat inside a tray at the bottom.
- Use two lumps of plasticine to make the tray stand upright.
- Use plasticine to fix the two candles, as shown in the photograph. Make sure that they are halfway from the front edge of the tray.
- Fix the card over the tray using sellotape. Leave a 5 cm gap at the top and bottom.
- Light the candles using a lighted splint.
- Predict what might happen to smoke from the straw if the straw were placed near the gap at the bottom.
- Now light the wax straw and test your prediction.
- When you have finished, record and explain your observations in a diagram.

Investigation A

## Investigation B

- Place the balloon over the neck of the conical flask.
- Place the flask in a bowl of hot water and leave it there for about 5 min.
- Observe what happens.
- Put the same flask into a bowl of ice and water and notice what happens this time.
- Use the words 'expand' and 'contract' to explain your observations.

Follow the plan

Investigation B

Investigation C

## Investigation C

- Put a jar into a refrigerator and leave it for 20 min.
- Set up the apparatus as shown in the picture.
- Put the lid on the jar in the refrigerator, then take the jar to the apparatus.
- Remove the lid and carefully pour the cold air into one of the bags.
- What have you discovered about cold air?

# Wind is moving air

The Earth is heated by the Sun's rays. The Earth then acts like a radiator and heats the air just above it. The warm air rises and cold air moves in to replace it. Cold air sinks because it is denser than warm air. As a result of all this, the air in the atmosphere is constantly moving.

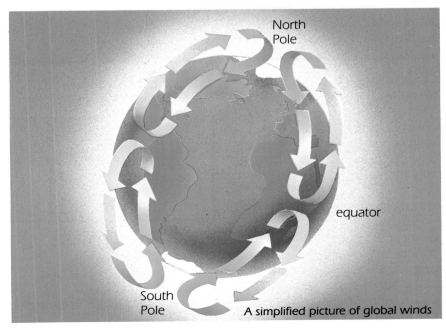

# Sea breezes

Have you ever noticed that the seaside sometimes can be windy on warm, sunny days? This is because the air above the land becomes warmer faster than the air above the sea. This makes the air above the land rise and the cooler air over the sea moves in to take its place.

A cycle of air movement is set up. This cycle is called a **convection current**.

# Global winds

A similar convection current is set up on a global scale. Air above the equator is hot and air above the poles is cold. Therefore, hot air over the equator rises and moves farther from the equator. It cools down high in the atmosphere and begins to sink again.

The air in our atmosphere is several kilometres high. This air has weight. The effect of the air pressing down on us is called **air pressure**.

Wherever air sinks, the air pressure becomes 'high'. Wherever air rises, the air pressure becomes 'low'. Usually the air pressure at the equator is low, as air rises there.

■ What is the air pressure likely to be at the poles?

During the day, the warm air above the land rises, and air flows in from the sea. This is called a sea breeze. At night, the sea cools more slowly than the land. The warm air above the sea rises, and air flows to the sea from the land. This is a land breeze

North Pole

equator

South Pole

A simplified picture of global winds

**83**

# Water all around us

Two-thirds of the Earth's surface is covered by water.

Some of this water evaporates because of the Sun's heat. This evaporated water is in the air all around us, but we cannot usually see it (unless it is misty or foggy).

If the air containing water vapour rises, it cools and condenses into clouds. Cold air cannot hold as much of the evaporated water as warm air, so the water vapour turns into liquid water droplets. Look at the figures in the table above.

Most of the Earth is covered with water, as this photograph from space shows. Africa and Saudi Arabia can be seen through the clouds

| Air temperature | Maximum amount of water that 1 m³ of air can hold |
|:---:|:---:|
| 10°C | 9 g |
| 30°C | 30 g |

Notice how cool air holds less water than warmer air.

The water in clouds comes down as rain when the tiny droplets join together to make larger drops.

Droplets that are too heavy to stay in the clouds fall to Earth, and end up in rivers, seas and oceans. Thus, we have a never ending cycle which we call the **water cycle.**

**WEATHERWATCH**

# The water cycle

■ Explain what is happening at **A, B, C, D** and **E**.

# Hot and sticky

The word humidity describes how much water vapour there is in the air. When the humidity is high, there is a lot of water vapour in the air and we feel sticky. It is often hot as well because hot air can hold much more water vapour than cold air. Cobalt chloride paper is a useful indicator of the presence of water (vapour).

■ Collect three pieces of cobalt chloride paper. Find out what happens when you wet one piece under the tap, when you breathe on another piece, and when you leave the third piece in the room.

■ What happens to the cobalt chloride paper in the presence of water? Does the amount of water make any difference?

■ Plan an investigation to find out about the humidity in three seaside resorts. The resorts are:
**resort 1**, hot and near the sea
**resort 2**, warm, near the sea
**resort 3**, cold, near the sea.

You can use the following items:
● stop watch
● three pieces of cobalt chloride paper
● three boiling tubes
● three paper clips to hang the cobalt chloride paper over the mouth of the boiling tubes
● hot water
● cold water

■ Carry out your plan and record your observations.
■ Write a report of your findings about humidity in each of the three resorts.

# The daily prediction

Once all the available information has been collected from weather stations, computers forecast the weather to come. This is then examined by a meteorologist, and the forecast presented by TV, radio and the newspapers.

## Weather maps

Weather maps usually have the following features:

*Isobars*
These are lines of equal air pressure drawn on a map. Pressure values are given in millibars. The closer the **isobars** are to each other, the more windy it is. Winds tend to move along the lines of isobars.

*High and low pressure areas*
In the northern hemisphere, winds move clockwise around **anticyclones** or high pressure centres, and anticlockwise around **depressions** or low pressure centres. In the UK in summer, high pressure areas are usually associated with fine weather and low with unsettled weather. In the winter, low pressure areas tend to mean wetter weather, whereas high pressure is associated with colder, dryer weather. You should look at spread 3.6 to remind yourself about the different airstreams.

*Fronts*
These occur when large masses of warm and cold air meet. Belts of cloud and rain are usually found along the whole length of a **front**. There are three types:
- warm fronts bring in warm air
- cold fronts bring in cold air
- occluded fronts, which are a type of combined front.

## Presenting a weather forecast

You are going to work in a production team to produce and present a TV weather forecast.

■ Decide who is going to do the following tasks from your team: direct the team's work; present the forecast in front of the camera; prepare the weather maps (two people are needed); research the weather forecast.

Your map should show the current weather situation.

■ Your task is to describe the weather now and to prepare and present a forecast for tomorrow. You may use **data sheets D3.12a and D3.12b**.

■ Your production should last 1 min 30 s and be informative, accurate and clearly presented.

**'Three, two, one ... on air!'**

■ When the other production teams give their forecasts, you can assess their presentations out of five in a table, like the one below.

You will not be able to complete the last column until tomorrow.

■ When you next watch the weather forecast on television, think about how much modern technology has been used in its preparation, from weather stations in the Atlantic Ocean to computer programming in the Meteorological Office, and the live transmissions broadcast to your home.

HIGH

| Team | Was the timing right? | Amount of information delivered | Was it clearly presented? | Was the forecast accurate? |
|---|---|---|---|---|
| 1 | | | | |
| 2 | | | | |
| 3 | | | | |
| 4 | | | | |
| 5 | | | | |

# 4.1 | Floating and flying

## Move it!

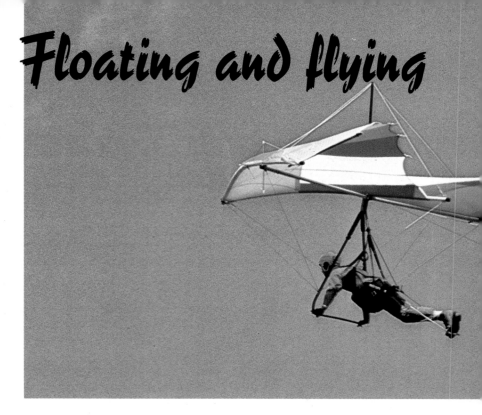

Have you ever wondered why it is that some things float and others don't?

When a boat floats, two **forces** act on it. One force acting on the boat is **weight**. Weight pulls the boat down. The second force is called **upthrust**. This is a force pushing upwards on the boat. Normally, the weight is balanced by the upthrust.

Although it may seem strange, similar ideas apply to a boat on water, to an aeroplane in the air and to a car on the ground!

Keeping opposing forces in balance is just as important for the hang glider as it is for an aeroplane – if it wants to remain in the air!

The more effectively the downwards force of the hang glider's total weight is balanced against the upwards force, (lift) the longer it will stay airborne.

Thor Heyerdahl's raft was called *Kon-Tiki*, after a legendary ruler of the ancient Inca kingdom of South America

## Float a raft

A raft is a simple kind of boat. An explorer called Thor Heyerdahl believed that in the past people might have travelled across the Pacific Ocean on rafts from South America to Tahiti. In 1950, to try and prove his hypothesis, he and five friends travelled 6920 km across the Pacific on a balsa wood raft like the one in the picture below.

As an aeroplane moves through the air, the shape of its wing means that there is an upwards force called **lift** acting on it. This force just balances the downwards force of the aeroplane's weight.

■ Discuss what you think would happen if the lift force was reduced.

The weight of a car is exactly balanced by an upwards force called the **reaction**, produced by whatever surface the car is on.

Record

■ Use kitchen foil to make a raft.
■ Devise a way to load and test the raft.
■ What is the greatest load your raft will carry without sinking?
■ Devise a way to report the results of your tests, including how you loaded the raft.
■ Write a letter to Thor Heyerdahl explaining to him the best way to load the food and provisions for his expedition. In your letter, you should explain the reasons why his raft will float if he loads it in the way you suggest.

89

# How does it go?

Have you ever tried rowing a boat on a lake or river?

■ Discuss with your friends how you felt after rowing.

Moving a boat (or anything else) needs **energy**. In the case of the rowing boat, you provided the energy, which is why you felt tired afterwards. You were the energy source.

■ The boat in the picture below does not have oars. What is its energy source?

One of the oldest sources of energy drives these yachts.
What is it?

## Fuel

Some boats have engines to make them move. Engines need **fuel** as the energy source. What is the usual energy source for a boat engine?

Most modern ships use fuel oil. For ships, this has many of the advantages that petrol has for the motor car.

■ Discuss what these advantages might be.

A few large ships such as aircraft carriers and some submarines use nuclear fuel as an energy source. A small amount of fuel will last for a long time, so the ship doesn't have to come into harbour to refuel. A submarine, therefore, can stay hidden under the water for a long time.

**MOVE IT!**

How does the force of the wind affect the movement of a raft? These children have set up a simple experiment to find out

## Sailing boats

We have seen that we can make things that float and sink, but how can we get a raft to move?

■ Look at the picture of the raft on spread 4.1.
■ How do you think the force of the wind and the direction of the wind will affect the movement of the raft?
■ Make an hypothesis about the effect of the wind on the raft. Remember: an hypothesis must contain a reason.

■ Plan an investigation to test the hypothesis you have made. (Use the 'exploration machine' to help you.)
■ Show your teacher your plan and then carry out the investigation. Your teacher will show you how wind power will be provided during the activity.
■ Record your observations. Was your hypothesis correct?

91

# Going faster!

So far, you have been investigating how sailing rafts move through the water. Most modern boats are not raft-shaped, however.

- Look at the three boats in the picture.
- Discuss with your friends which moves through the water most easily, and why?
- You may have found it difficult to answer the question. The picture does not show a fair test. Why is that?

When an object moves and rubs against something else, a force called friction acts to slow the object down.

- Discuss how friction acts to slow your bicycle when you stop pedalling.

Moving boats are also affected by friction. Friction between the boat and the water tends to slow the boat down.

- How do the people who build boats try to reduce friction?

**MOVE IT!**

## Measuring forces

■ Use newtonmeters to measure the force needed to do the sort of tasks shown in the pictures.

■ Make sure that you use the correct newtonmeter for each different task.

■ Make a table to record your measurements.

Record

95

# Inside structures

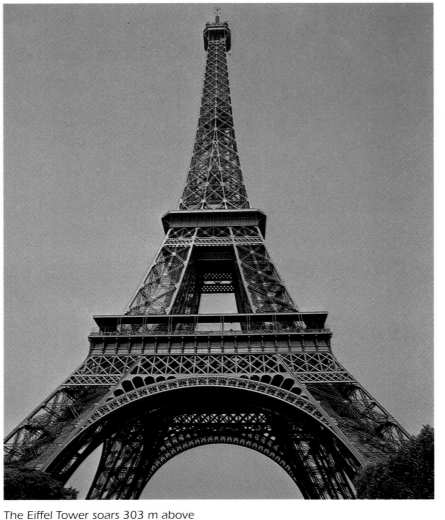

It may be hard to believe, but all materials change shape when forces act on them. The changes that take place in a block of concrete or a steel girder are often so small that they are difficult to see with the eye.

■ Discuss with your friends what happens to the Eiffel Tower when the wind blows.

If an object changes shape when a force is applied and then goes back to the same size and shape when the force is removed, it is said to be **elastic**.

The **load** on the beam in the picture on the opposite page is the weight of the elephanr plus the weight of the beam itself. The load causes the beam to bend. Inside the beam:

● the top surface is pressed inwards, or is in **compression**
● the centre is least affected
● the bottom surface is pulled outwards, or is in **tension**.

■ Discuss this with your teacher.

The Eiffel Tower soars 303 m above Paris, France. It was built in 1889 by Alexandre Eiffel, a brilliant engineer

Something being pressed inwards is said to be 'in compression'.
Something being pulled outwards is said to be 'in tension'

**MOVE IT!**

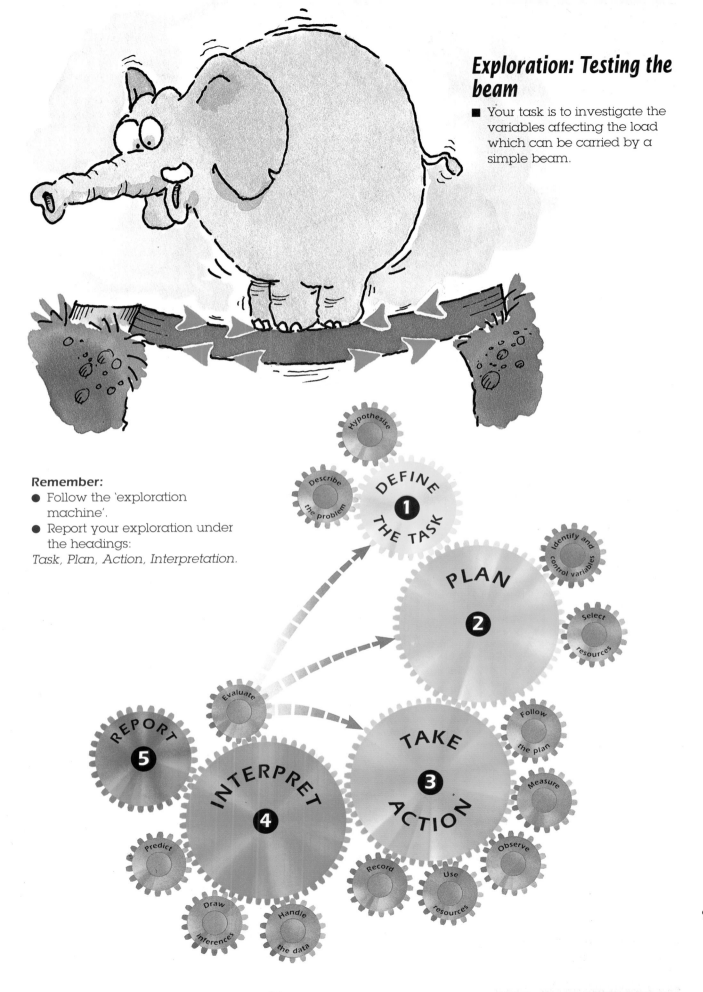

## Exploration: Testing the beam

■ Your task is to investigate the variables affecting the load which can be carried by a simple beam.

**Remember:**
● Follow the 'exploration machine'.
● Report your exploration under the headings:
*Task, Plan, Action, Interpretation.*

Hypothesise

Describe the problem

**DEFINE THE TASK** ❶

**PLAN** ❷

Identify and control variables

Select resources

Evaluate

**REPORT** ❺

**INTERPRET** ❹

**TAKE ACTION** ❸

Follow the plan

Measure

Observe

Predict

Record

Use resources

Draw inferences

Handle the data

97

# Bridging the gap

Engineers and scientists use special words to describe how forces act on and affect structures such as bridges.

If we push a structure, then we say it is in compression. The forces are trying to squash it.

If we pull a structure, we say it is in tension. The forces are trying to stretch it.

## Types of bridge

Here are three types of bridge.
*Beam bridge*
Lay a plank of wood across a stream and you have a beam bridge. If the beam is supported at each end by uprights which project towards the middle, it is a cantilever bridge.
*Arch*
Quite small blocks of stone are shaped carefully to fit tightly together. All the stone blocks in an arch are in compression. Stone is good at resisting compression.
*Suspension bridge*
Cables are used to support a flat deck (the road). The support cables pass over the towers and down to anchorages. The cables are in tension and the towers are in compression.

For a successful bridge, both the design and the choice of materials are important.

Beam bridge

Arch bridge

Suspension bridge

**MOVE IT!**

# AMAZING NEW MATERIALS FOUN[D]

English scientists today announced the discovery of two amazing new materials that could revolutionize the whole construction industry.

Runour has been rife in the manufacturing industry for some years now heralding the arrival of exciting new materials. In fact, it has been said that its properties are so unusual that the ... will probably never

... Switzerland to discuss some of the many fundamental problems inherent in the industry's most important building materials. Weight, flammability, strength, resitance to wear and tear were just some of the areas covered with reference to specific materials.

scientific specialist should be approached and entrusted with the task of developing new materials that would meet the ever increasing demands of both politicians and environmentalists.

So after a decade of toil by the scientists, the secret's finally out - announced with all the razzmatazz of the launch of a new political party. Called nottoc and ittehgaps, the new materials show an increase in torsional strength of more than 200% while reduc...

... convention agreed

## Testing materials

Scientists have discovered two new materials but not enough is known about their suitability for building bridges! The materials are nottoc and ittehgaps.

- In the next activity, you will use nottoc and ittehgaps to build a bridge. Try to plan and carry out compression and tension tests on both the new materials.
- You will need to measure and record the forces used to test the materials.
- Write a full report of your tests on **data sheets D4.6a and D4.6b.**

REPORT

# Two bridges across the Forth

The picture shows the cantilever bridge which spans the Firth of Forth in Scotland. When completed in 1890, the bridge carried two railway lines across the Firth of Forth and spanned 1631 m. A workforce of 4500 took 7 years to build it. There were 57 fatal accidents during construction. The design used 50 000 tonnes of steel and 8 million rivets. More than 54 tonnes of paint are needed. It takes three years to paint, and when painting is finished it is time to start again.

When a new road bridge across the Forth was needed in the 1960s, engineers were more skilful and had better materials to use. They were able to design and construct a suspension bridge next to the cantilever bridge. The towers rise to 158 m and support cables made of many thousands of steel wires. Only 250 people were employed to build this bridge. It used only 30 000 tonnes of steel.

■ Look carefully at both photographs.
■ Discuss the differences between the two bridges. What shape is used on the rail bridge and why? Which parts of the suspension bridge are in tension and which in compression?

The 1890 Firth of Forth bridge

100

MOVE IT!

# Build a bridge

- Your task is to design and construct a bridge to span the length of a laboratory storage tray. You may choose any design of bridge.
- There must be at least 4 cm clearance under the bridge for a boat to pass through.
- It must support a load of 10 N (a 1 kg mass) at mid-span.
- Your design must be cost-effective (good value for money).
- Work out how much your bridge has cost to build.

### SEDU
**BUILDING SUPPLIES LTD**

#### Price List

Nottoc .............£2000 per metre
Ittehgaps ........£1000 per length
Hire of............£500 per day or
glue gun                part thereof
Glue sticks.......£2000 per stick
Card ................£5000 per sheet

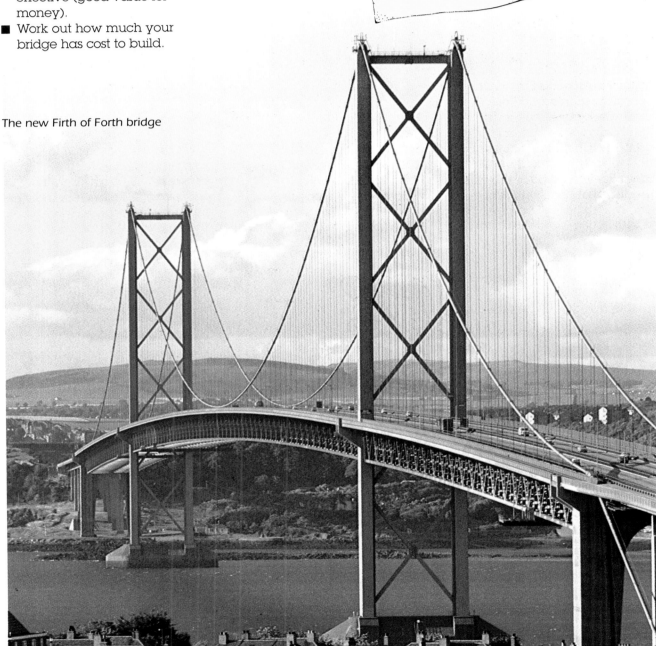

The new Firth of Forth bridge

# On the move

People have always had a need to travel.

- Discuss with your friends some reasons for this. In your discussions, you should consider the sorts of vehicles that people used in the past as well as those we use today.
- What are the differences between early vehicles and modern vehicles?

## Speed

Modern vehicles travel much faster. The **speed** of boats and cars is measured in different units. Car speedometers in England and the USA are usually marked in miles per hour (mph). See if you can find out what units are used to measure the speed of boats. In France and most other countries in the world, speed is measured in kilometres per hour (km/h).

To calculate the speed of something, we need to know two things about it:

- the distance it travels
- the time it takes to travel that distance.

If we measure distance in miles and time in hours then the units of speed will be miles per hour. If we measure distance in metres and time in seconds, what would the units of speed be?

All vehicles should have a means of stopping quickly. How do you do this on your bicycle? The speed you are travelling affects the time and distance it takes to stop. If you need to stop quickly, you have to pull the brake lever much harder to exert a larger stopping force.

**MOVE IT!**

# Traffic survey

- Your task is to plan and carry out with a friend a traffic speed survey near your school. You need to know how far the vehicles travel and the time it takes them to cover this distance. It may be helpful to use trees or lamp posts as markers for this activity.

- Select appropriate measuring instruments for the task.
- Draw a table like the one below and record your measurements for each vehicle that passes.
- To work out speed, use a calculator to divide distance by time:

speed = distance ÷ time

- Fill in the last column of your table with your results.
- Write a report on your traffic speed survey.
- Read the information on **data sheet D4.8** and answer the questions on it.

Use resources

| Type of vehicle | Distance between markers (m) | Time to travel between markers (s) | Speed (m/s) |
|---|---|---|---|
|  |  |  |  |

## SAFETY ⚠️

When you carry out your survey, be sure that you are safe from all the traffic. Make sure that your teacher knows exactly where you will be at all times.

## Did you know?

The world's fastest car is the rocket-powered *Budweiser Rocket*. On 17 December 1979, it was driven by American Stan Barratt at over 1190 km/h (739 mph), which is faster than the speed of sound.

Traffic in Hong Kong

Think about a person riding a bicycle. Where does the energy to move the bicycle and rider come from?

■ Discuss this with your friends. When you pedal a bicycle, you apply the pushing force to the

pedal, yet the force is needed at the wheel to make the bicycle move along. How does the energy you supply get from the pedal to the wheel?

In cars, energy is supplied in the form of petrol or diesel. A

pipe takes the liquid fuel to the engine, where it is burnt to release the energy to turn the wheels. This energy is passed through a series of gears (in the gearbox) and along metal shafts (driveshafts) to the wheels.

## MOVE IT!

You may have used technical Lego to make models move. You may have needed to move energy from one part of your model to another. To do this you will have used gears, rubber bands or shafts.

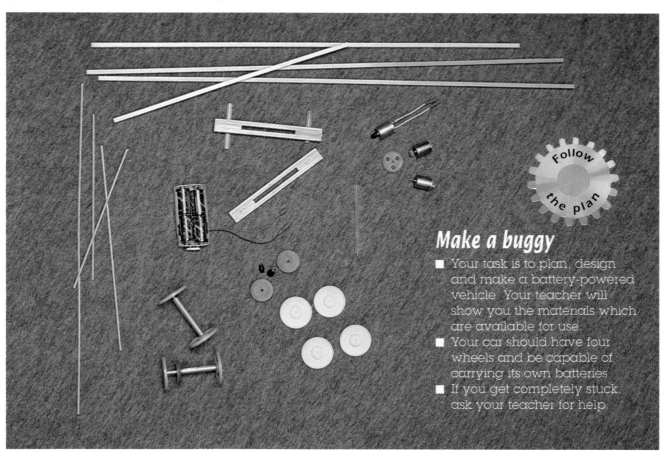

## Make a buggy

- Your task is to plan, design and make a battery-powered vehicle. Your teacher will show you the materials which are available for use.
- Your car should have four wheels and be capable of carrying its own batteries.
- If you get completely stuck, ask your teacher for help.

# That sinking feeling

Have you ever tried to ride your bike in soft sand, snow or mud? Maybe you have been in a car that has become stuck in soft ground. When people have to drive on snow, they often let some of the air out of the tyres of the car. What does this do to the shape of the tyre and to the area of the tyre in contact with the ground? Why doesn't a skier sink into soft snow?

■ Discuss with your friends what might be the advantage of letting some air out of car tyres when driving on snow.

■ Look at the picture on the next page. Why doesn't a bulldozer sink easily into soft ground?

**MOVE IT!**

A giant bulldozer moves easily through soft mud

## Buggies investigated

- Your task is to investigate the behaviour of your buggy.
- Raise questions which you would like to investigate.
- Choose one of your questions and devise a way to investigate it.
- Carry out your investigation.
- Adapt your vehicle so that it can cross a tray full of sand.
- Report your investigation.

Describe the problem

# Turning forces

Forces which try to turn things, such as the force of the wind on the boat and the crew's weight, are called turning forces. When you open a door, you use a turning force on the handle. We call this the **effort**. The force you overcome is known as the **load**. The distance from the effort to the turning point (or **pivot**) affects the size of the force needed to do the job. In the picture, the weight of the boy being lifted is the load.

- Look at the photograph.
- Discuss why the boat does not capsize, even though the wind is trying to push it over.

- How have the boat crew increased the distance of the effort force from the turning point?
- Look at the pictures below with your friends and decide in each case where the effort force, load and pivot are. One picture has been labelled to help you.

## Lift a friend!

- Use a long piece of wood and a piece of broom handle to set up an arrangement like that shown in the picture.
- Apply an effort force at the end of the plank. This time, apply the effort force closer to the pivot.
- Describe what you noticed in trying to lift your friend. Where is it easiest to apply the force successfully?

**MOVE IT!**

effort

load

pivot

# Going up?

Astronaut Harrison Schmitt collecting rocks on the Moon during the Apollo 17 mission in 1972

The launch of Apollo 11 – the first mission carrying people to the Moon taking off from the Kennedy Space Center, USA, on 16 July 1969

Every planet and star has its own different force of gravity. The size of the gravity force depends upon what the planet is made of and its size. The force of gravity on the Earth is about six times bigger than on the Moon.

- Discuss with your friends the direction in which gravity would act if you were on the surface of the Moon.
- Report your group's ideas to the class.

Remember the story of Isaac Newton and how watching an apple fall helped him to make an hypothesis about a force called gravity? What would happen if gravity suddenly ceased to exist?

Which way would an apple fall if you lived in Australia? You might never have been to Australia but even so, you can still be pretty sure of your answer! Will the answer always be the same wherever you live on the Earth's surface or will it vary from place to place?

You may have seen someone using a plumbline when hanging wallpaper. What force is pulling the plumbline straight down towards the floor? Gravity does the same thing to the apple and the plumbline. It always pulls things in the same direction, towards the centre of the Earth.

So far, we have been talking about gravity on our own planet.

**MOVE IT!**

## 3, 2, 1 ... lift off!

- Use a large plastic drinks bottle to make a water rocket.
- Look at the sketch of the rocket. The pump increases the **pressure** of the air in the bottle; eventually, the bottle escapes from the bung.
- Use the diagram to help you assemble the rocket.
- Use a bicycle pump to increase the pressure of the air inside the rocket.
- Investigate the effect of different amounts of water in the rocket.
- Describe what happens to the rocket when more water is added to it.
- What happens to the rocket when all the water has come out of it?
- Draw a diagram to show the path taken by your rocket.

**SAFETY** ⚠️
The rocket takes off quite suddenly. Stand clear while it is launched.

plastic bottle
air
bicycle pump
rubber bung
water
one-way valve
plastic tubing

111

# Living and changing

## A changing environment

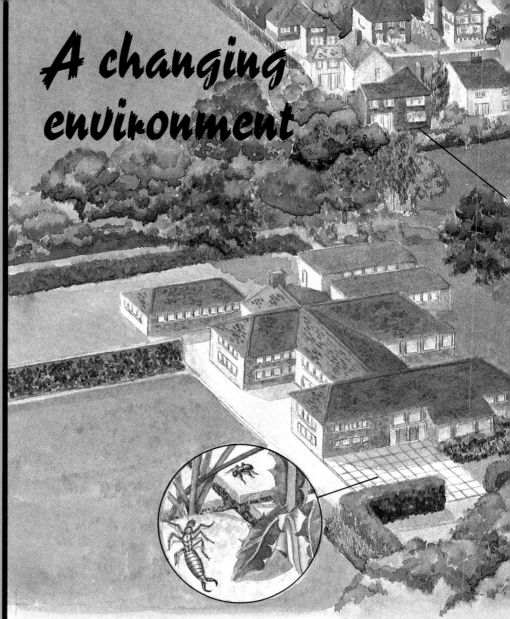

The environment is the area where plants and animals (including humans) live. There are lots of particular places, or localities, in the environment. The grounds around your school provide many examples:
- the playing field
- lawns
- flower beds
- the cracks between paving slabs.

Animals and plants depend on each other in many different ways. For example, plants can give shelter to animals. Some types of bird build their nests in hedges, others prefer to use trees, while skylarks nest on the ground in open meadows.

## Competition for life

Living things are in competition with each other for the things necessary for life. These include light, water and soil space. Can you think of any others? The winners in this competition live longer. Plants which don't receive enough light or animals which don't obtain enough water from their environment, for example, may die out completely and become extinct – either locally or worldwide.

- Can you think of some examples of animals or plants which have become extinct, or are perhaps in danger of becoming extinct?

# Investigate the school grounds

In your first activity, you will explore your local environment – the grounds around your school.

### Investigations outside the laboratory

- Work in groups of two or three.
- Record the names of at least 10 different living things that you have found in the school grounds, but which you have never noticed before.
- Look for and collect 10 leaves each from a different plant in the school grounds.
- Make a list recording the names of any animals with wings that you can see around the school.

### Investigations inside the laboratory

- Sort your leaves into these two groups according to their appearance: put leaves of similar lengths into the same group; regroup the leaves depending on their shape (e.g. oval leaves, rounded leaves, leaves with smooth edges, leaves with 'saw-toothed' edges etc).
- Sort the list of winged animals that you have already seen and recorded into the following two groups: animals with backbones, or vertebrates; animals without backbones, or invertebrates. (These animals sometimes have hard outer cases called exoskeletons which protect the soft inner parts.)
- What effect do you think the largest leaves will have on any plants and animals living underneath them?
- Are most of the plants that you have found similar in one way which you can see easily?
- Did you find one group of plants which were very different in appearance? If so, what was the difference?

No environment remains the same all the time; there is continuous change. Sometimes, these changes take place very slowly. Other changes take place once or several times within a 24-hour cycle.

- Can you think of some of these environmental changes which occur every day?

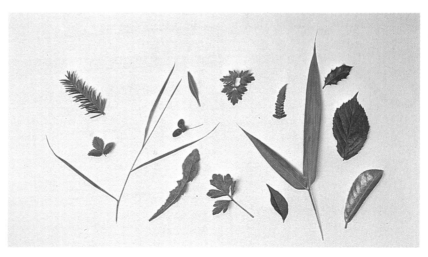

# Biological keys

No-one can remember the name of every animal or plant. There are far too many of them. However, scientists frequently need to be able to identify different living things.

Searching through books full of descriptions and pictures would take a long time. It is much quicker to use a biological key to help solve this problem.

A biological key asks a series of questions about the organism which is being studied. The route which you take through the steps of a key depends upon the answers to the questions.

Eventually, the key leads to the name of the organism.

Using the external features of a plant or an animal, it is possible to put plants into their major groups: non-flowering or flowering; and animals into their major groups: invertebrates or vertebrates.

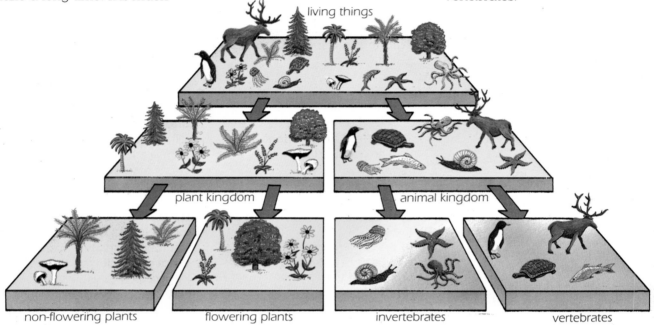

living things

plant kingdom        animal kingdom

non-flowering plants        flowering plants        invertebrates        vertebrates

■ Look at these vertebrate animals and then see if you can use the key below to name them.

| **Key** | | | |
|---|---|---|---|
| **1** | **A** | (If) the animal has scales (go to) | **2** |
| | **B** | (If) the animal does not have scales (go to) | **3** |
| **2** | **A** | (If) the animal has dry scales (it is a) | **Lizard** |
| | **B** | (If) the animal has wet scales and fins (it is a) | **Trout** |
| **3** | **A** | (If) the animal has feathers (it is a) | **Bird** |
| | **B** | (If) the animal has fur (it is a) | **Hare** |

**LIVING AND CHANGING**

## Using a key

On **data sheet D5.2** you will find pictures of various invertebrates.

■ Use the key below to find the names of these animals.

| A key to some common invertebrates | | |
|---|---|---|
| | | 4 |
| **1** A The animal has legs or tentacles | | 2 |
| B The animal does not have legs or tentacles | | Snail |
| **2** A The animal has a coiled shell | | 3 |
| B The animal has no obvious shell | | Earthworm |
| **3** A The body is made up of segments | | Flatworm |
| B The body has no segments | | 5 |
| **4** A The animal has three pairs of legs | | 7 |
| B The animal has more than three pairs of legs or tentacles | | Housefly |
| **5** A The animal has one pair of wings, large compound eyes, short antennae | | 6 |
| B The animal has two pairs of wings | | Damselfly |
| **6** A The animal has a slender body which is longer than the wings | | Stonefly |
| B The body is shorter than the wings, the tail has two prongs | | 8 |
| **7** A The animal has eight legs or tentacles | | 9 |
| B The animal has more than eight legs | | Octopus |
| **8** A The animal has eight tentacles and has an unsegmented body | | Mite |
| B The animal has eight legs and a segmented body | | Crab |
| **9** A The animal has five pairs of legs, the front two ending in claws | | 10 |
| B The animal has more than five pairs of legs | | Centipede |
| **10** A There is one pair of legs to every body segment | | Millipede |
| B There is more than one pair of legs to every body segment | | |

## Making a key

■ Your task is to make a key to identify four animals of your own choice. For each animal, make a list of its features, for example does it have fur or scales, how many legs does it have? Use these features to write a key which other people could use to identify your animals.

# Who eats whom?

Some animals only eat plants, for example the caterpillars which live on cabbage leaves. These animals are called **herbivores**. Some animals eat other animals. Blackbirds and thrushes, for example, eat caterpillars, snails and worms. These animals are called **carnivores**. Animals which eat both plants and animals are called **omnivores**.

■ Think about the variety of foods you eat. To which group do humans belong? We have a special name for animals which hunt and feed on other animals. They are called **predators**. The animals which are eaten are called the **prey**.

The way in which predators, prey and green plants fit together in an environment can be shown as a food chain.

**An example of a simple food chain in the garden:**

> **green plants**
> eaten by
> **herbivores**
> eaten by
> **carnivores**

**greenflies**
eaten by **ladybirds**

**rose bush**
plant juices sucked
out by **greenflies**

## The hunting game

This game involves a series of hunts made by a pride of lions which are preying on a population of antelopes living in Moremi National Park.
You will need **data sheet D5.3.**

Follow the plan

### Rules of the game

■ Work in pairs. One person takes the part of the lions and the other takes the part of the antelopes.

■ Antelopes start with a population of 30. They hide in the squares of the National Park. Mark 30 squares lightly with a pencil to show their distribution. Do not let your partner see where they are.

■ Lions begin with a pride of three lions.

■ Lions hunt by naming a number from 1 to 50. If there is an antelope in this square, it is rubbed out because the hunt is successful. If there is no antelope in this square, the hunt is unsuccessful. Lions must keep a record on rough paper of successful and unsuccessful hunts.

■ A round of hunting means that each lion has one guess at where an antelope is hiding in the Park.

**LIVING AND CHANGING**

- After each round of hunting, the number of successful and unsuccessful hunts is added up and the populations are changed like this: for every successful hunt, one extra lion is added to the pride; for every two *unsuccessful* hunts, one lion is removed from the pride due to starvation; two extra antelopes are added after every round because of reproduction. (Remember to mark these on your plan of the National Park.)
- The results must be recorded after every round in a table like this:

| Round of hunting | Number of lions | Number of antelopes |
|---|---|---|
| Start | 3 | 30 |
| 1 | 2 | |

### Example

Imagine a game where, after 3 rounds, there are 7 lions and 22 antelopes. In the next round there are 4 successful and 3 unsuccessful hunts. Because of the successful hunts, 4 extra lions are added but 1 lion is removed because of the unsuccessful hunts.

The new lion population = $7 + 4 - 1 = 10$

In addition, 4 antelopes were killed but 2 are added every round due to reproduction.

The new antelope population = $22 - 4 + 2 = 20$

- Continue for up to 20 rounds of hunting.
- At the end of the game: Has the balance between predator and prey changed during the game? Did the skill of the hunters affect the relationship?

# Same or different?

No two individuals of the same type, or species, are exactly the same. Even identical twins have some differences. Biologists call the differences between individual animals or plants **variations**. The overall variation between individuals is caused by both genetic and environmental variation.

## Genetic variations

These differences are present at the start of life. They are inherited from the parent plants or animals and can be passed on to the next generation. For example, the colour of the eyes of a fruit fly depends upon the colour of the eyes of the parent fruit flies.

- Are there any similarities or differences, for example hair colour, which have been inherited throughout the members of your family?

In what ways are these twins similar? In what ways are they different?

Which plant grew in the dark?

## Environmental variations

These differences are not present at the start of life but are caused by conditions in the local environment. Examples of such conditions include varying amounts of light, water supply and differences in the available soil minerals.

For example, a plant grown in the dark will be very different from a plant grown in full sunlight, even if both plants were grown from cuttings taken from the same parent. Both plants inherited exactly the same features, so in theory they should be identical. They look different because different environmental conditions have caused variation in their growth.

## Why is variation important?

Variation is important for survival. A species in which every individual is identical and which is perfectly adapted to its environment will be successful. If, however, there is a sudden change in environmental conditions, for example a change from a wet to a dry climate, then the species will probably die out in that locality.

If some individuals are slightly different from the rest and are able to tolerate the new, drier climate, the species will survive.

## Selective breeding

Variation is also important in selective breeding programmes. Horticulturists try to find individuals which have useful characteristics, for example short stem height in wheat plants. The short-stemmed individuals can be used to produce offspring with even shorter stems.

This kind of work has led to the development of dwarf wheat varieties. These have saved money for farmers because they do not blow over in strong winds.

## Measuring variation

Fitzlyker Ltd, the famous glove manufacturers, want to start a new line of children's safety gloves for use in school laboratories. They have decided to concentrate on the 10–12 year old market.

The production manager believes that children of this age all have hands of about the same size. Therefore, it is only necessary to make one size of glove to fit every child.

The research director thinks that the amount of variation in hand size is so great that the company will have to make gloves of several different sizes.

Fitzlyker Ltd have decided to call in a firm of consultants to discover who is correct.

■ Imagine that you are the consultants. Your task is to investigate if there is a variation in hand size. You will, therefore, be able to recommend what size of gloves should be made.

■ Use the 'exploration machine' to help you. Make an hypothesis about variation in hand size – an hypothesis is an idea with a reason. Plan how you will investigate any variation in the size of hands of the children in your class.

■ After making a plan, carry out your investigation. What measurements will you have to take? How will you record your results?

*Hypothesise*

### Interpreting your results

■ When you have recorded your results, draw a bar chart using the axes shown below.

■ Discuss your results with the others. Is there much variation of hand size in your class?

■ Was your hypothesis correct? Would you advise Fitzlyker Ltd to make only one size of glove or a range of sizes?

■ Write a letter to the production manager of Fitzlyker Ltd recommending how many sizes of glove the company should make. In your letter, you should give: details of how you carried out your investigation; all the reasons, including your results, which support the recommendations you have made.

# 5.5

# A place to live

If you went on a long journey from the Arctic to Antarctica, you would pass through many different environments. You could go from the polar ice-cap, through northern pine forests, grasslands, alpine meadows, deserts and many other areas.

While on this journey, you would notice many changes in the environment. The climate would range from the permanently frozen Arctic or Antarctic to the steamy heat of the tropical rain forests.

The landscape would include mountains and valleys, flat plains, gently rolling hills, rivers, lakes and seas. The soils would also vary widely in both depth and richness.

You would notice that, as you passed from one type of environment to the next, the types of plants and animals in the area also changed.

The animals, such as antelopes, which live in the African Savannah (grasslands) would be out of place in the Arctic Circle, and polar bears are certainly not found in Africa.

■  Why do you think this is?

Parts of the world which have similar environments have similar plants and animals. The plants which you would see high up in the colder regions of the Alps are similar to those found in the Arctic Circle. They are called Arctic–Alpine plants.

In later activities, you will be investigating whether different types of animals are found in different environments around your school. You will be thinking about why animals and plants live where they do.

# Investigating soil animals

- Your task is to investigate the numbers and types of animals in soil from two different localities: under short, trampled grass; under leaf litter or dead wood.

## Investigations outside the laboratory

- Work in groups of two or three.

In each area:
- Clear the surface of the soil and take a small sample. One trowel-full should be enough.
- Place the sample in a labelled plastic bag. Take it with you to the laboratory.

- Record the temperature of the soil both at the surface, and at a depth of 5 cm. You will have to use a special soil thermometer or an electronic sensor.
- Write a brief description of the location.

*Always treat living things with care and return them to their habitat at the end of the lesson.*

## Investigations inside the laboratory

For each soil sample:
- Count and record the total number of soil animals found.
- Use the key on **data sheet D5.5** to try to identify the animals and count the number of each type of animal. Record your observations.
- Mix a small amount of soil with some distilled water in a test-tube. Filter the suspension using a funnel and paper. Collect the filtrate in another test-tube. Test the pH of this filtrate using a strip of universal indicator paper. Record your results.
- Was there a difference in the total number of animals found in the two different soil samples?

- Were there differences in the types of animals found in each area?
- Discuss with your partner(s), the possible reasons for any of the differences that you have discovered (e.g. soil pH, temperature, shading, or any other cause that you can think of). Record your ideas.
- If you were to sample the same area next week, next month or even next year, would you expect to get the same results? Explain the reasons for your answer.

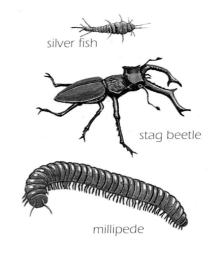
silver fish

stag beetle

millipede

earthworm

slug

Using a soil thermometer

# 5.6 Features for survival

The fennec fox, which lives in the Sahara desert, is adapted for life in hot climates. Its large ears act as radiators and give off excess heat

To survive, animals and plants must be adapted to the locality in which they live.

Plants living in the cracks in a pavement must grow as close to the surface of the concrete as possible. What would happen to a plant if it continued to increase its height on a busy pavement with many people passing by?

A similar danger faces plants growing on a lawn which is mowed regularly. Successful broad-leaved plants such as daisies and dandelions survive by growing close to the soil. They often grow as a tightly packed group of leaves called a rosette.

## Survival in deserts

Animals and plants which live in deserts have many special adaptations allowing them to live in a hot, dry environment.

Desert plants have long roots to obtain water from deep below ground. They have a shiny layer of wax over their stem to reduce water loss and small leaves, or only spines. These spines also reduce water loss because they have a small surface area.

■ In what other ways do spines help desert plants to survive?

Cacti are a typical group of plants which live in deserts.

Mammals that live in deserts often have large ears. Some of the body heat produced during movement and digestion is lost from these large surfaces.

■ Do you think that mammals which live in the Arctic and Antarctic will also have large ears and long tails?

## Camouflage

The colour of the animal can also be important in helping it to survive. Colours and patterns which help an animal to merge into its surroundings are called **camouflage**. Camouflage helps some of the prey animals to hide from their predators.

■ How do body colours help the hunters to survive?

Some animals actually change their colour at different times of the year. The willow grouse and ptarmigan are two game birds from northern Europe. They grow white feathers for the winter. The stoat and the Arctic fox are two predatory mammals which live in the same geographical region. They grow white fur.

■ What is the advantage of this seasonal colour change for creatures which live in or near the Arctic Circle?

Woodcock fledglings camouflaged among leaves

## Design a creature

You have looked at some ways in which animals and plants are adapted to survive in different places, including the environment outside your school.

The picture below shows a different environment – a deep, dark swamp on the imaginary planet of Kulmarnus. The climate is hot and steamy. There is hardly any oxygen in the atmosphere. The short 'day' is equal to four hours on planet Earth. Darkness at night lasts three times as long.

■ Your task is to design a 'life form' (an animal or plant) which would be well adapted for survival on Kulmarnus.

■ Make a large, fully labelled drawing of your 'life form'. Any adaptations or special features for survival should be explained clearly.

# The changing seasons

No environment always stays the same. In North Africa, the Sahara desert has the highest recorded 'shade' temperature anywhere on Earth, 58°C. At night, temperatures in deserts drop sharply and they become very cold.

On Earth, changes occur in temperature between day and night and also throughout the year during the four seasons: winter, spring, summer and autumn.

Plants and animals respond to seasonal changes in many

*Many animals hide away to sleep, or hibernate, during the cold winter months*

different ways. Deciduous trees lose their leaves in autumn. Most deciduous trees have 'broad leaves' which have a large surface area.

■ How would a heavy fall of snow affect the branches of deciduous trees, if they kept their leaves throughout the winter?

## How animals adapt

Some animals, including British bats and North American bears, sleep or hibernate through the cold months of winter. Other

animals avoid unfavourable seasonal conditions by travelling or migrating from one part of the world to another.

■ Can you think of any examples of vertebrates and invertebrates which migrate?

In addition to these longer-lasting seasonal changes, the regular changes of day and night take place every 24 hours.

Animals which are active by day are called **diurnal**, for example humming birds. Animals which are active at night are called **nocturnal**. British bats hunt at night.

■ What sort of differences would you expect in the external appearance of diurnal and nocturnal animals?

**LIVING AND CHANGING**

The Negev desert in Israel during the dry season (below). The same scene after rain (right) is full of colour as flowers bloom

## Exploration: What conditions do seeds require to germinate?

Many European flowering plants blossom in the spring and summer. The seeds from these flowers don't always start growing, or **germinate**, immediately. They often lie inactive, or **dormant,** in the soil through the cold winter months.

In other parts of the world, desert plants survive as seeds through months of drought, only germinating after the next rainfall. In fact, new plants grow and flower so quickly after rain that the desert is said to 'bloom'. These quick-growing plants, which have only a short life cycle while the desert is moist, have a special name. They are called **ephemerals.**

■ Plan and carry out an exploration to discover the effect of temperature on seed germination. Your teacher will give you the seeds to test.

**Remember:**
● Follow the 'exploration machine'.
● Report your exploration under the headings:
*Task, Plan, Action, Interpretation.*

■ What temperature would you recommend if you were designing a seed bank to store seeds of the same type as you have tested? Give a reason for your answer.

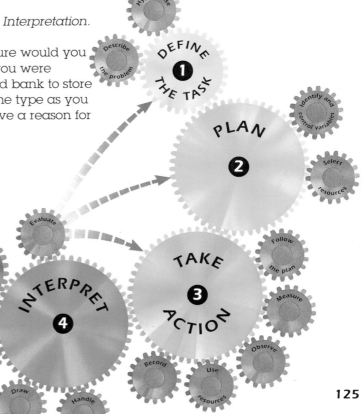

125

# Sources of pollution

Most of the things people do alter the environment in some way or other. Some of these changes can be harmful to the lives of all plants and animals.

## Sea and air pollution

Changes might be easy to see. For example, the black crude oil washed on to a beach from a leaking tanker at sea is obvious.

Other changes caused by humans are less obvious. One of the changes that we can't see is the release of carbon dioxide into the atmosphere.

■ Why do you think that we can't see carbon dioxide gas?

The damaging effects of escaping oil quickly become obvious, but effects of the release of too much carbon dioxide take longer to show. Both types of damage to the environment are known as **pollution**.

Pollution is often the result of the careless things people do or their attitude. 'It's someone else's problem,' they say. However, we all breathe the same air which circulates around the world in the atmosphere. The water in the seas and oceans is also a shared natural resource. Therefore, the poisoning of the sea and the air affects us all.

## Land pollution

The land can also be polluted. Everyone produces rubbish such as paper and cardboard packaging, empty glass bottles and metal cans. Some of these materials get spread about at refuse tips or are deliberately dumped in the countryside by thoughtless people. Do you always put your empty crisp packets in a litter bin?

■ During the next break or lunchtime, look around the school grounds to see if this type of pollution is a problem in your local environment.

What evidence of pollution is there in the photograph?

**LIVING AND CHANGING**

# Detecting and preventing pollution

Pollution occurs in the air, in water and on land. Your task is to investigate an example of each type of pollution.

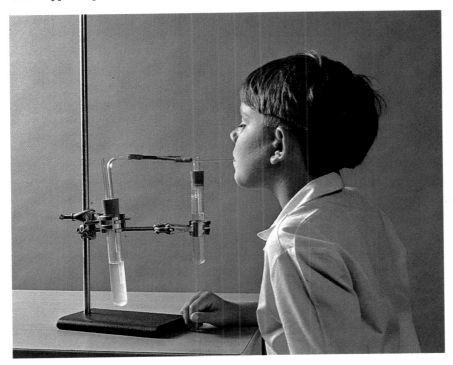

## Air pollution: investigating carbon dioxide

The amount of carbon dioxide in the atmosphere can be increased by:
- animal and plant respiration
- burning fuels such as coal, wood and petrol.

The test for carbon dioxide is that it turns lime water milky.

■ Does the air we breathe out contain more carbon dioxide than the air we breathe in? Use the apparatus shown above to investigate this question. Record your observations.

■ Does a burning candle produce carbon dioxide? Investigate this problem using the apparatus below and record your observations.

## Water pollution: investigating the effects of oil

The most common type of oil pollution is caused by mineral oil. This oil is extracted from the ground.

■ Take three 250 $cm^3$ beakers and put 100 $cm^3$ of water into each one. Pour oil on to the water to a depth of 5 mm. What happens?

■ What effect do you think a layer of floating oil will have on the plants and animals living in a rock pool on the beach or under the water in a canal?

■ How can you disperse or sink this oil?

■ Add a few drops of washing-up liquid to the first beaker. What happens?

■ Drop powdered chalk on to the film of oil in the second of your beakers. What happens to the oil?

■ If you add sawdust to the film of oil in the third beaker, what happens? Would you be able to scoop up this oil and sawdust mixture from the surface of polluted water?

■ From your experimental results, which of these three methods would you recommend to prevent the spread of oil pollution on areas of water?

■ Write a report of your findings.

## Land pollution: unwanted rubbish

■ In groups of two or three, discuss if there is a litter problem in your local environment. If you think there is, what can you do to solve the problem? Are more litter bins the answer?

■ Can you educate the polluters about the damage they are doing to the environment?

■ Would you ban eating snacks at break time?

Brock Wood

River Idle

N

A 300

city

Foxley village

Linden Grange Park

A 314

**Map of Foxley Mound area**

The county of Ruralshire lies in central England. The county contains a major city where more jobs and houses are needed, together with shopping and leisure facilities for the people. The local authority Planning Department has identified that Foxley can provide these.

Foxley is a medium-sized village set in high quality agricultural land. Two main roads run through the village, creating a traffic problem. The local authority believes a by-pass will solve this problem.

In return for permission to build houses, shops and the industrial park, the developer will provide a leisure complex and by-pass.

## Objections to the plan

However, there have been many objections to the plan from existing residents of Foxley. They are worried about the size of the new development, the increase in traffic and noise, and the loss of part of Linden Grange Park. Linden Grange house is of great historic and architectural interest. The park contains many trees which are specially preserved and, with Brock Wood, provides an important habitat for plants and animals.

A public inquiry is held for everyone to put forward their views both for and against the Local Plan.

# The public inquiry

- In groups of five, your next activity is to take part in the public inquiry into the Foxley Mound Local Plan. Decide who is going to play each of these roles:

**Inspector** – controls the inquiry

**District Planning Officer** – explains and supports the plan and reports on views put forward to the Secretary of State for the Environment

**Chairperson of Richly Investments** – supports the plan

**Conservationist** – objects to parts of the plan

**Residents' Committee Representative** – objects to parts of the plan.

- When you have decided on your roles, each person must read the information provided for their particular part on **data sheet D5.9**.

- The Inspector will open the inquiry. You may wish to take notes as other people are speaking or record the inquiry using an audio tape recorder or camcorder.

- After the inquiry has taken place and everyone has had the opportunity to speak, a *complete* report has to be written, based on the evidence for and against the plan. The Secretary of State for the Environment decides whether the plan will be accepted, altered or rejected. It is most important, therefore, that your record presents the all evidence as accurately as possible.

- In your report, you should include the following information:
  - the main changes which will occur in the environment, if the original plan goes ahead unaltered;
  - if you support the plan, you must say why you think it is a good idea;
  - if you think that the plan should be changed, you must explain what these changes are and why you think they are important;
  - if you think the plan should be rejected, explain why.

**Foxley Mound Local Plan**
This map shows the planning proposals for the by-pass, new industry, houses, hypermarket and leisure complex. A new 'green area' will separate Foxley from the city.

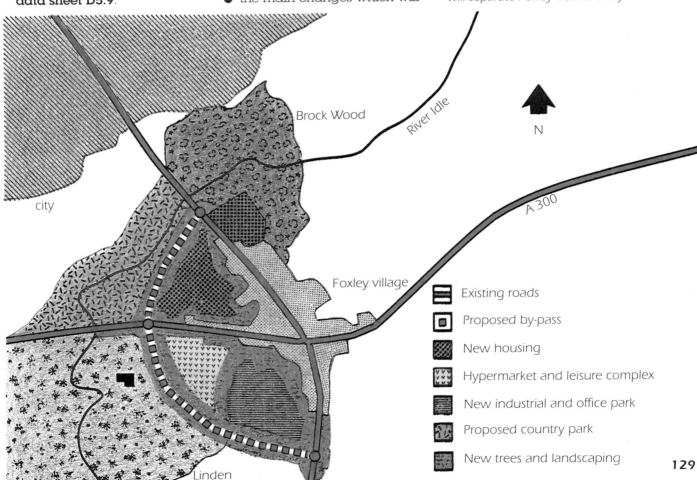

Existing roads

Proposed by-pass

New housing

Hypermarket and leisure complex

New industrial and office park

Proposed country park

New trees and landscaping

# A better future?

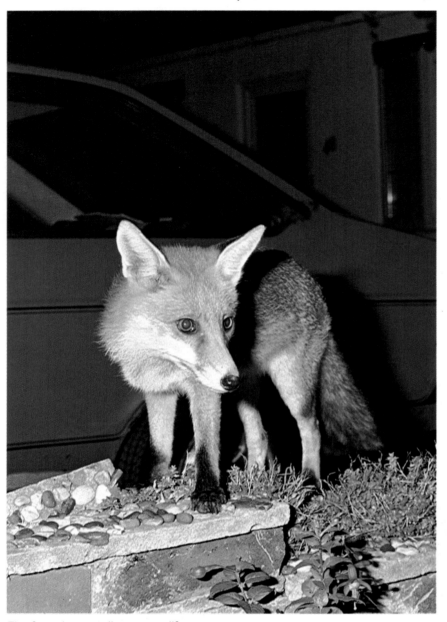

The fox adapts easily to town life as cities spread into the countryside. Unfortunately not all animals are as adaptable

You have seen that the environment doesn't remain the same all the time.

Some changes take place every 24 hours, for example night turns into day. There are also slower changes over several months. In Britain, the weather in each of the four seasons is different, for example. Such patterns of change are not the same everywhere.

## Altering the balance

You have also investigated how plants and animals depend on each other. In particular, you have seen how the way in which animals feed and hunt can alter the balance in their environment.

However, the biggest changes to the environment are brought about by humans.

■ Can you think of some examples where human activities completely alter the environment?

Is there a balance between the human activities which are good for the environment and those which damage it?

## What can you do?

There are many things you can do at school and at home to improve the environment. You will look now at a few examples which would help to ensure a better future for everyone.

130

## In your school

- Design, produce and distribute posters to inform and educate about environmental problems. Are there other types of pollution requiring attention as well as those investigated in spread 5.8?
- Take part in school competitions such as those organised by Shell Better Britain and the World Wide Fund for Nature.
- Organise the recycling of valuable resources to help the environment: collect and recycle old newspapers; collect and recycle aluminium cans; set up a bottle bank to recycle glass.
- Construct a chequerboard arrangement of paving slabs and different soil types such as sandy soil, clay, loam and rapidly draining pebbles. You can then grow colonies of specially adapted plants.
- Build and/or maintain a school pond or a wild garden.
- Give an account of what you have done.

How does using products like these help the environment?

REPORT

## Outside school

- Join local groups and societies which undertake practical environmental projects and publish further information in newsletters and magazines, for example: the Royal Society for the Protection of Birds; the local County Naturalist Trust and their junior wing, 'Watch'.

Conservation work can be fun!

# Glossary

**accelerate**
getting faster

**acid**
a sour-tasting, corrosive chemical; an acid solution has a pH of less than 7

**air pressure**
the weight of air over a certain area of the Earth

**algae**
simple, very small plants

**alkali**
an alkaline solution has a pH of greater than 7 and can neutralise (cancel out) an acid

**alloy**
a mixture of two or more metals

**anemometer**
an instrument for measuring wind speed

**anticyclone**
an area of high air pressure

**artery**
a blood vessel which carries blood away from the heart

**atoms**
the tiny particles that matter is made of

**bacteria**
a microorganism made up of a single cell

**Beaufort scale**
a scale used to measure wind speeds

**biomass**
the total mass of living things in an environment

**camouflage**
colours and markings on an animal similar to its surroundings

**capillary**
a narrow blood vessel with thin walls which allow oxygen and dissolved food to pass through

**carbohydrate**
a type of food which provides energy

**carbon dioxide**
a colourless gas found in small amounts in the air

**carnivore**
an animal which eats other animals

**cell**
the tiny unit of which all living things are made

**cell membrane**
the thin skin around a cell

**cell wall**
the rigid wall around a plant cell

**chlorophyll**
the green pigment in plants which absorbs light energy from the Sun during photosynthesis

**chloroplast**
the parts of a plant cell that contain chlorophyll

**chromatography**
a way of separating soluble pigments

**classify**
to group together things according to their properties and features

**compression**
a squashing or pushing force

**condensation**
the process of changing a gas into a liquid by cooling

**convection current**
an upwards movement of warm air

**cumulonimbus cloud**
a large storm cloud that can cause hail and thunder

**cytoplasm**
the clear, jelly-like substance found inside cells

**density**
the amount of matter in a certain volume

**depression**
an area of low air pressure

**digestion**
the process by which food is broken down and made soluble so that it can pass into the blood

**diurnal**
active during the day

**dormant**
inactive

**effort**
the force used to lift a load

**elastic material**
a material that returns to its original shape when any force acting on it is removed

**energy**
the ability to do work

**environment**
the area where animals and plants live

**enzyme**
a substance produced by living things which changes the speed of chemical reactions, such as those occurring during digestion

**ephemeral plant**
a plant which has a very short life

**evaporation**
the change of a liquid to a gas without boiling

**exoskeleton**
a skeleton which is outside the body

**fat**
a food which provides energy

**filter**
a very fine strainer used to separate insoluble solids from liquids

**filtrate**
the liquid that passes through a filter

**food chain**
a series or line of living things, each of which is the food for the next in line

**food pyramid**
a diagram showing which animals feed on plants and which on other animals

**food test**
a test to determine the content of foods

**force**
a push or a pull

**friction**
a force that slows down moving objects that rub against other objects

**front**
a zone where cold and warm air meet, often causing cloud and rain

**fuel**
a substance which releases energy on burning

**genetic variation**
the differences between individuals of the same type which are present at birth

**germinate**
to start growing into a plant

**gravity**
a force of attraction between objects caused by their mass, which pulls objects closer together

**herbivore**
an animal which feeds on plants

**humidity**
a measure of how much water vapour is in the air

**hypothesis**
a reasoned guess

**indicator**
a chemical that changes colour when added to an acid or alkali

**insoluble**
does not dissolve

**invertebrate**
an animal which does not possess a backbone

**isobar**
a line joining places of equal air pressure on a map

**lift**
the upwards force on, for example, the wings of an aeroplane due to its movement through the air

**load**
the weight carried by a beam, or the force overcome by a lever or other machine

**localities**
the particular places where plants and animals live

**mass**
the amount of matter in an object, measured in grams and kilograms

**matter** or **material**
what everything is made of

**meteorology**
the science of climate and weather

**microorganism**
a very small organism that can only be seen through a microscope

**mineral**
an essential substance for growth of living organisms

**neutral solution**
a solution which is neither an acid nor an alkali

**newton**
the unit of force

**newtonmeter**
an instrument used to measure the size of forces in newtons

**nocturnal**
active during the night

**nucleus**
the part of a cell which controls everything going on in the cell

**omnivore**
an animal which feeds on plants and animals

**organ**
a group of different types of tissues with a particular job to do

**organ system**
a group of organs

**organism**
a living plant or animal

**pathogen**
an organism that causes disease

**pH scale**
a scale of numbers that shows how strongly acidic or alkaline a chemical is

**photosynthesis**
the process by which plants make their food

**pigment**
a substance that gives colour to things

**pivot**
a turning point

**pollution**
damage to the environment caused, for example, by poisonous materials

**precipitation**
rain, sleet, hail or snow

**predator**
an animal which hunts and eats other animals

**pressure**
the force acting over a given area

**prey**
the animals hunted and eaten by predators

**property**
a feature used to describe and identify a material

**protein**
a substance found in some food which is used for growth and repair

**reaction**
a force that is the same size but in the opposite direction to another force

**residue**
the solid which a filter separates from a mixture

**respiration**
the process by which energy is produced from simple food substances

**satellite**
an object in orbit

**solubility**
how easily something dissolves

**soluble substance**
a substance that dissolves

**solute**
the solid that dissolves in a solvent to make a solution

**solution**
the mixture obtained by dissolving a solute in a solvent

**solvent**
the liquid that dissolves a substance

**species**
a group of animals and plants that can breed among themselves

**speed**
the distance covered in a given time

**states of matter**
the different forms of matter: solid, liquid, gas

**Stevenson screen**
a container holding thermometers and other weather measuring instruments

**tension**
a stretching or pulling force

**thermometer**
an instrument for measuring temperature

**tissue**
a group of the same types of cells

**upthrust**
the upwards force acting on an object in a liquid or gas

**vacuole**
a fluid-filled sac inside a cell

**variation**
the differences between individuals in a group of the same animals or plants

**vein**
a blood vessel which carries blood to the heart

**velocity**
speed in a given direction

**vertebrate**
an animal with a backbone, and a skull surrounding its brain

**vibrate**
move rapidly back and forth

**virus**
a tiny organism that lives in the cells of plants and animals

**vitamin**
a substance found in food which is needed in small amounts for health

**volume**
the space taken up by a solid object, liquid or gas in three dimensions

**water cycle**
the way water circulates in nature: evaporates from rivers, lakes and seas; rises into the atmosphere forming clouds; rain falls from the clouds; returns to the rivers, lakes and seas

**weight**
the downwards force pulling an object towards the Earth

# Index

# Acknowledgements

The co-ordinators would like to acknowledge the help and support given to them in the development of *New Horizons: science 5–16* by their teaching and advisory colleagues in West Sussex. They would like to thank the following schools for providing valuable assistance in the production of this book: Buckingham Middle School, Shoreham; Boundstone Community College, Lancing; Imberhorne School, East Grinstead; Oathall Community College, Haywards Heath; St Paul's RC School, Haywards Heath; Thomas Bennett Community College, Crawley.

The authors and publishers would like to thank the Meteorological Office for permission to reproduce the continental air flow diagram (p 74) and Usborne Publishing Ltd for permission to reproduce the 'eating machine' illustration (pp 42-3) from *How Your Body Works*.

## Photographic credits

*t = top   b = bottom   c = centre   l = left   r = right*

**Cover**: Allsport UK

8*b*, 8*t*, Science Photo Library; 9*t* ZEFA; 10*l*, 12, 14/15, 17, 18*tl*, 18*tr*, 18*cr*, 19, 20*t*, 20*b* Trevor Hill; 21 ZEFA; 22/23*c*, 23*br*, 24/25*t*, 26, 27 Trevor Hill; 28*t*, 28*b* ICI; 29*t* Syndication International; 34/35, 37 Allsport UK; 38 Planet Earth Pictures; 40/41 Trevor Hill; 44/45 ZEFA; 44*l* Planet Earth Pictures; 44*r* Science Photo Library; 45*l*, 45*r* ZEFA; 48*b* Trevor Hill; 50 Science Photo Library; 51, 52, 53 Trevor Hill; 54*t* ZEFA; 54/55*b* Trevor Hill; 57*l* Science Photo Library; 57*r*, 58 Trevor Hill; 60*b*, 61*t* Science Photo Library; 62, 63*r* Trevor Hill; 64, 65*tr* ZEFA; 65*tl* Bruce Coleman; 66 Chris Fairclough Colour Library; 69 Science Photo Library; 70, 71*t* Trevor Hill; 71*b* Science Photo Library; 72/73 Frank Lane Picture Agency; 75*t* ZEFA; 76 Bruce Coleman; 77*b* International Centre for Conservation Education; 78*t* Frank Lane Picture Agency; 81, 82*t*, 82*b* Trevor Hill; 84 ZEFA; 86*l*, 86*r* Trevor Hill; 88*t* ZEFA; 88*b* Allsport UK; 90 ZEFA; 91 Trevor Hill; 96 ZEFA; 99*b* Trevor Hill; 100 Chris Fairclough Colour Library; 101 ZEFA; 102*t* Mansell Collection; 103 ZEFA; 104 Allsport UK; 105*t* , 105*c*, 105*b* Trevor Hill; 106, 107*t* ZEFA; 107*b* Trevor Hill; 108*t*/109*t* ZEFA; 110*l*, 110/111*t* Science Photo Library; 113*b* Trevor Hill; 118*t* Chris Fairclough Colour Library; 120*tr* ZEFA; 120*tl*, 120*cl*, 120*cr*, 120*b* Planet Earth Pictures; 121*b* Trevor Hill; 123*t* Planet Earth Pictures; 125*l*, 125*r* Frank Lane Picture Agency; 126 ZEFA; 127*t* Trevor Hill; 130 Planet Earth Pictures; 131*t*, 131*b* Trevor Hill.